# FURY OF A HIGHLAND DRAGON

DRAGONFURY SCOTLAND BOOK 1

COREENE CALLAHAN

0 9 8 7 6 5 4 3 2 1

*For Grandpa—thank you for all the stories. You gave me a passion for Scotland, our ancestral home. I loved it then and still love it now.*

# 1

CAIRNGORMS, SCOTLAND: THE HIGHLANDS

STANDING on top of his favorite cliff, Tydrin leaned forward to peer over the edge. Moonlight illuminated the weathered face, caressing sheered stone, slipping deep into narrow crevices, reaching toward the heart of the mountain. He squinted against the glare, protecting his light-sensitive eyes, and stared at what most considered certain death. A straight drop. A cascade of ice and snow. Nothing but the snarl of jagged rock for a thousand feet.

Nice.

Neat.

Tidy tied up in a chaotic twist.

A fitting end for someone, but not him. Jumping wouldn't bring relief, much less undo what he'd done. Or erase the past.

Self-reproach tied a knot in the center of his chest. Barbed and brutal, the individual threads pulled, making him ache from the inside out. Not surprising. It was that time of year. Again. Like always. Inevitable as the changing tide, the seasons turned, blowing Nordic winds into arctic bluster and strands of hair into his face. Tydrin shook his head, denial rising as he raked the dark mass out of his eyes. January 7th. Bloody hell, he hated the date. Despised its annual occurrence. Despaired as one month spun into the next, dragging him closer to winter and the reckoning.

Penance. Forced restitution. A guilty conscience that never abated...

Or let him rest.

His gaze on the thick curl of gathering storm clouds, Tydrin shoved his hands into the front pockets of his favorite jeans. The yawn of a large cave behind him, he settled in his usual spot, bare feet cradled by well-worn grooves, shoulder propped against the rock wall. Ice pressed against his arm. The chill woke his dragon half, sharpening his senses as he stared out into the void. Into nothingness. Into the snowy swirl of midnight and the beauty of the mountain lair he shared with the other members of his pack.

Dragonkind hidden in the wilds of the Scottish Highlands.

Smack dab in the midst of human society.

Amid a mountain range so inhospitable most never ventured anywhere near it.

Tydrin's mouth curved. Cairngorm, a beautiful beast wrapped in ragged terrain and subzero temperatures. An excellent home. Perfect cover for his kind.

Blackened by time, scarred by harsh weather and covered in snow, individual peaks rose and fell, dropping into valleys, angling into sheer stone faces, shooting skyward to touch the hand of God. He huffed. *God.* Right. It was so much bullshite. Faith. Hope. The need to believe in a supernatural force that watched him from above, holding the world—and all in it—in the palm of *His* hand. Apathy drilled deep, leaving a bad taste in his mouth. The dogma smacked of foolishness—of archaic beliefs set inside ancient parameters that no longer held sway.

A shame in many ways.

He could use a little faith right now. A touch of what humans held in such high regard.

But even as he searched, hope rising hard, none came. No great burst of inspiration. Not a whisper of relief either. The crush of inevitability compressed the cradle around his heart. Tydrin ground his molars together. The harsh sound echoed inside his head, killing the quiet, heightening his grievance, laying the blame at his feet.

Lucifer lash him and get it over with. Would it never end? Would he ever be able to let it go? He wanted to forget. Longed to learn how and leave history where it lay, buried in the past, but—

"You still here?" The deep voice drifted from the rear of the cave.

Tydrin tensed. Well, shite. Talk about bad luck. And even less solitude.

With a sigh, he glanced over his shoulder.

A pale purple gaze met his.

Tydrin swallowed a growl and eyed the bastard with enough balls to sneak up on him. "Aye."

"Thought tae find you gone by now."

The statement tightened his chest. He should be *gone*. Ought to be in dragon form and airborne, making his annual trip to the human cemetery. That he still stood cliff-side told the tale better than any explanation ever would. But then, dread—and the promise of penance—had a way of stalling a male's forward progress. "You thought wrong."

Cyprus, commander of the Scottish pack, raised a brow. "Wool gathering, are ye?"

He shrugged, refusing to add fuel to the fire. His

older brother didn't need to hear about the guilt plaguing him anymore than he wanted to talk about it. So instead of answering, he changed course, deviating into the only subject guaranteed to turn his brother's attention. "Any word from Vyroth?"

Eyes shimmering in the gloom, Cyprus left the shadows and walked into the open. Moonlight fell across his face, illuminating aristocratic features. Deceiving in many ways. Sure, his brother looked like royalty—played the part from time to time as well— but anyone who knew the male understood the truth. Cyprus might be controlled, but he was also the loveliest sort of lethal. Was a stone cold killer when warranted, just like the rest of his pack.

A hard glint in his eyes, Cyprus stopped alongside him. "No word yet. The little prick. 'Tis a fine time for him tae disappear."

Tydrin's lips twitched, finding humor in the name calling. Particularly since *little* in no way described Vyroth. "Tempted tae call him out when he gets home?"

Cyprus snorted. "I could use the fight, and my twin never disappoints."

True enough.

Irrefutable, in fact, 'cause well...if Cyprus epitomized vicious, Vyroth tripled the effect, then multiplied it by ten. Aye, the two might be identical in appearance, but sharing a womb before birth didn't make them the same. The twins differed in personality: one night, the other day. Steadfast and even, Cyprus excelled at leadership, providing the stability and guidance each member of the pack required. But Vyroth? Tydrin stifled a snort. Shite, the male was the picture of unpredictable. Toss in unreliable. Mix it up with a bad attitude and...uh-huh. No way around it.

Vyroth did as he pleased, always had—to hell with the rest of the world.

Which explained his absence over the last few weeks, didn't it?

Unconcerned by protocol, Vyroth always left without a word. No head's up. No see-yah- later. Nothing but silence and an empty bedroom. He and Cyprus had come to expect it. Both of them understood the male's restlessness, his need to get away, explore the world, be one with his dragon half. His most recent trip, however, concerned Tydrin. It wasn't like his brother to stay away so long. A couple of days—a week at most? Certainly. But over a month without any word at all? He frowned. Nay. Such overt disregard wasn't Vyroth's MO.

"Any leads?"

"Vyroth is still tae far away for me tae track, but..." His brother rolled his shoulders, working out the kinks. "I can feel him. He's still alive."

"Good." Tydrin exhaled in relief. His brother's claim made sense. Closer than most siblings, the twins possessed a special bond. The cosmic link coupled with identical DNA allowed Cyprus to connect to their brother's life force over great distances. A handy skill. The best, really, with Vyroth MIA more often than not. "Let me know when he makes contact."

A furrow between his brows, Cyprus nodded.

"Later then." Onward and upward. He couldn't put it off any longer. "Donnae expect me before dawn."

Pushing away from the wall, Tydrin stepped closer to the cliff edge. Cold stone brushed the soles of his feet. He ignored the chill. As a fire dragon, his temperature ran south of hot. Which meant he went shirtless most of the time. Tonight was no exception. Bare skin steaming, he flexed tense muscles, preparing to leave his perch. Time to shift into dragon form and get airborne. Avoiding what must be done wouldn't make it go away. He knew from experience. Had tried time and again to forego the annual trip.

To no avail.

Self-recrimination refused to let him ignore it. Call it impulse. Call it compulsion. Call it duty touched by honor. The exact cause didn't matter. He needed to pay homage. The small show of respect served as an excellent reminder: of his loss of control, of his crime, and the consequences of a violent temper.

"Hey, Tydrin?"

The concern in his brother's tone drew Tydrin tight. His hands curled into fists, he waited for Cyprus to continue. He knew what was coming. Same argument, different year. But no matter how many times he explained, Cyprus didn't understand. Instead, they went round after round, the quarrel quiet, but forever the same.

"'Tis time tae put it behind you, brother," Cyprus said, his tone so reasonable Tydrin wanted to rip his head off. Let his fists fly. Do some damage. Hammer his sibling into the ground for interfering. Yet again. "It cannae be undone, lad. And twenty years spent punishing yourself is twenty years tae many."

Untrue.

He deserved to be punished. Over and over. Again and again. Forever, if necessary, for what his loss of control had wrought.

A human couple lay dead, cold in their graves.

Bad enough, but even worse was the lass. The wee innocent who'd been robbed of a happy future with loving parents. His fault. One hundred percent his doing. Now his eternal cross to bear.

Tydrin exhaled a stream of frigid air. The white

cloud puffed in front of his face. He shook his head. So many years ago, and still sight of the house burning and the dead humans inside ate at him, burdening him with a heavy sense of responsibility.

Young and foolish.

Both described him well—at least, back then.

Now, though, after years of training, he knew better and understood more. Could curb the rise of his explosive temper by taking a deep breath and choosing another path. One that resulted in peaceful endings, not mayhem and murder.

"Tydrin," Cyprus murmured. "Brother, listen tae me—let it go."

Tydrin didn't answer.

He leapt off the ledge instead.

Ignoring his brother's curse, he freefell toward the jagged rocks below. Bitter wind blew his hair back. The smell of midnight melded with a hint of heather, soothing him with the scent of Highland moors. Halfway down, he shifted, hands and feet turning to claws, body lengthening beneath black purple-tipped scales, the hum of magic in his veins.

Wings spread wide, he banked into a tight turn. A brisk north-easterly lifted his bulk, gifting him with an updraft. He sliced between two vertical rises. Shale broke away, tumbling down the cliff face. The rattle echoed over mountain peaks, dipped low into valleys as he rotated into a rolling flip, powered up a cloaking spell, and flew east.

Half an hour later, he rocketed past the city limits. Into the heart of Aberdeen. Into a city steeped in a history rich with feuding clan chieftains and incompetent kings. The place he called home. But as he scanned the deserted cobblestone streets, following the inky, serpentine curve of the River Don, he wondered for the first time if that was true. Was it really his home?

Tydrin frowned.

He didn't know anymore. Mayhap Vyroth was onto something. Mayhap a change of scenery would cure what ailed him. Mayhap the separation would bring clarity, enough to remedy the keen sense of restlessness he suffered, night in and night out...

Day after sleepless day.

Wheeling into a tight turn, he increased his wing speed. Frosty air rushed over his scales, bringing relief as bright streetlamps blurred into streaks below him. The smell of peat moss rose, smoke twisting from stone chimney tops. Grey wisps swirling in his wake, he leveled off, gliding over the small cottages and tiled rooftops west of town.

Almost there. Another minute and—

Ah, there it was...the source of his disquiet. His annual destination: Nellfied Cemetery, the last place he wanted to be, but knew he couldn't avoid.

Divided into three walled sections, the graveyard sat silent and dark, skeletal tree limbs as still as the world around him. He circled overhead. His night vision sparked, allowing him to see the smallest details.

Not that Tydrin needed it.

He knew the desolate place by heart. Had memorized every inch: the pale face of every tombstone, each gravel covered path, the open area behind a semi-circle of evergreens where he preferred to land. Folding his wings, he dropped through frigid air. His talons thumped down. Frozen blades of grass crackled in protest before flattening beneath his large paws. Razor-sharp claws cutting into the soil, he scanned the shadows. His eyes narrowed. Huh. Strange, but...

A tingle crawled over the nape of his neck.

Already taut muscle cranked a notch tighter.

He tilted his head and listened harder. Nothing. Not a whisper of sound, just an odd vibration in the air.

Gathering his magic, Tydrin held it a moment, then released it in a rush. His sonar pinged, casting a wide net, blanketing the area as he searched for the source. A buzz lit off between his temples. Tydrin bared his fangs on a silent snarl. Shite. Trouble. The kind he couldn't identify, but knew lay just beyond the thick copse of evergreens.

Somewhere close to the grave site he intended to visit.

Shifting from dragon to human form, he conjured his clothes. Jeans and leather jacket... check. Heavy-duty combat boots on his feet...double check. Senses seething on violent swirls... tick the last box. All systems go. He was ready to roll. Footfalls silent and pace even, he circled right, headed for the edge of trees, hunting for the threat.

"I'm sorry. So, so sorry."

The whispered words tapped along his spine. Unease, and something more—a *something* he didn't recognize—twisted his instincts.

The apologetic murmur came again.

Tydrin's brows collided. The voice belonged to a female. One whose cadence held no hint of a Scottish accent.

A hitched intake of breath, then, "I should have visited before now, and...I'm sorry. I know it isn't right, but I haven't been able to face it. To understand how it happened. Why it all went so wrong, and...God. This is way harder than I thought it would be."

The halting apology made him pause. Curiosity urged him to move closer. Unable to resist the pull,

Tydrin stepped from behind the cluster of evergreens and—

Stopped short.

Surprise stalled the air in his chest, strangling his next breath.

Feet rooted to the ground, he stared at the female. He blinked to clear his vision. Nothing. No change in his visual field and—bloody hell. It couldn't be. He must be seeing things. Must be imagining the impossible. But no matter how many times he forced himself to refocus, nothing changed. She remained front and center, kneeling in the dirt, head bowed, hands resting on her thighs. The submissive position drew him tight, messing with his ability to think for a second.

Tydrin shook his head.

The movement knocked brain cells into motion and...Good Goddess. Unbelievable. She was real. He wasn't imagining her. Or the radiating warmth frothing around her like sea foam.

Glowing bright blue, the female's aura lit up the space around her. Her bio-energy hummed and his dragon half woke, setting off a dangerous chain reaction. Bone-deep hunger punched through. His body came alive. His mind dulled, blocking out everything but her.

Long red hair pulled into a messy bun, she shuffled closer to the headstone. Mumbling another apology, she cleared debris away from the granite base. The task was one he usually preformed. On this date, every year when he visited. Right now, though, he didn't care about his mission.

Or about paying his respects.

Struck stupid by her, only one thought registered —a high-energy female here...in the heart of Aberdeen.

His brows collided.

Holy shite.

He was in trouble. Neck deep and sinking fast without any idea how to control his reaction. To be expected. He'd never encountered a HE female before, much less stood within touching distance.

Veritable unicorns in Dragonkind circles, HEs were the rarest of the rare. Females whose connection to the Meridian—the electrostatic bands that ringed the planet, nourishing all living things—was so powerful Dragonkind males fought to possess them. An archaic practice, mayhap, but...hmm, baby. With her less than ten feet away, he understood the compulsion. Biological imperative shoved him forward, lifted his feet, urging him to get closer. To touch. To taste. To discover what all the energy would feel like pressed against his skin.

Gaze glued to her, he took a second step. And then another.

Saliva pooled in his mouth.

Tydrin swallowed, combating the ferocious need, fighting for control, trying to reason with errant urges.

Logic didn't work.

Neither did threats.

Not surprising.

With his dragon fixated on her, he was past the point of negotiation. Arousal pushed to the forefront, upping the stakes, making his heart pound and his body throb.

His feet moved again without his help.

Frozen grass crunched beneath his boot treads.

The harsh sound stopped his forward progress.

He drew a deep breath, hoping more oxygen would spark his failing intellect. Frigid air rushed into his lungs. His brain reengaged, force feeding him a

shovelful of common sense. A plan. He needed one...
right now. Before he did something stupid—like scare
the ever-living shite out of the female. Not the best
way to go if he wanted to get close. And oh how he
yearned to, 'cause...aye. Now that he'd seen her, he
wanted to know—how she would taste, how she
would fit in his arms, how it would feel to be fed by
such powerful energy.

The thought cranked him tighter.

Excitement skittered down his spine. Tydrin tightened the leash on his control. He didn't want to
frighten her. The moment he did, she'd run scared,
and he'd lose his chance.

Which left him with two choices.

Option one—approach her here, in a deserted
cemetery, and hope for the best. Option two— wait for
her to finish, follow her home, find out everything
about her before engineering a chance meeting between them. Tydrin nodded. Aye. Definitely. A perfectly reasonable way to go. But even as he cemented
his plan of attack, temptation urged him to drop the
invisibility spell, step up behind her, and grab hold.
Wrapped her up. Take her home. Love her well.

His dragon half snarled, liking the approach.

He shut it down. The compulsion smacked of stupidity. Was witless in every way, and yet—

He ran his gaze over her again. A twig snapped.

The sharp sound brought his head around.

The female didn't hear it. Busy with the clean-up,
she soldiered on. No change in her posture. No spike
of alarm in her bio-energy. Just the scent of sorrow
and a desire to make something right. Dragging his
focus from her, he scanned the shadowed forest
edging the graveyard. His night vision narrowed, then

sharpened. A moment passed before he spotted the threat.

Two males. Both human. Dressed in dark clothing.

Eyes narrowed, Tydrin watched the lead man unholster his sidearm. Raising the gun, the asshole leveled it at the female. Aggression swelled. Catastrophic. Urgent. Lethal. The need to defend her detonated deep inside him. His dragon answered the call, begging to be set free. With a mental flick, he opened the cage, allowing the killer inside him to step out an instant before he moved.

Fuck option two.

Forget restraint. Table the safe and sound approach too.

Reasonable would have to wait. Goddess knew, he couldn't. Not with a female to protect and a couple of idiot humans to turf.

## 2

T HE CLIMB over the high stone wall almost killed her. The half mile trek across the cemetery in the dark hadn't helped much either. Not that Ivy Macpherson could afford to complain. Not after escaping with little more than the clothes on her back. She was alive and mobile, and no matter how screwed up the situation, she refused to take it for granted.

Gratitude surfaced along with her relief.

On her knees in the dirt, she bowed her head. A cold breeze flicked over the nape of her neck. She shivered and, closing her eyes, offered up a quick prayer. An inadequate way to say thank you maybe, but...

By God, she'd made it.

All right, so it hadn't been smooth sailing. She'd been lucky. So damn fortunate to have gotten out of Washington D.C. in one piece. Quick wits had helped. A friend with questionable business contacts had done the rest, providing fake ID, some cash, and a one way trip to the UK.

A rough ride by any standards. To be expected given the circumstances. The crew aboard the freightliner *Mary Frances* would never be called sweethearts. Or embody kindness.

She should know. After a week of hiding out on the open seas—of scrubbing pots, mopping floors, and dodging the cop-a-feel Captain—Ivy now understood the meaning of hard work. Manuel labor at its finest. Sexual harassment at its worst. Not a bit like her regular job. But then, the terrified and on the run couldn't be choosy.

Neither could a hacker accused of espionage by the US government.

Eyes riveted to the tombstone, Ivy coughed into her sleeve.

Public enemy number one. A fugitive on the run. *Wanted*. And not in the way she'd always imagined.

Her way involved a hot guy with dreamy eyes and serious bedroom skills.

The Feds' way involved a mug shot, a country-wide APB, and a trip onto their most wanted list. God. She brushed wayward strands of long hair out of her eyes. How screwed up was that? Very. So crazy she could hardly put it into words.

Regret tightened her chest.

The lockdown made her lungs spasm and... crapity, crap, crap. Here she went again, playing keep away with constricted airways.

Stupid lungs.

Frigging asthma.

It reared its ugly head at the worst times.

She coughed again, willing her windpipe to open. The band of pressure compressing her ribcage eased. Not a lot. Barely enough for her to stave off oxygen deprivation, but well...hell. No need to get dramatic about it. She was accustomed to her condition, so forget about complaining. Time to toughen up and grow a pair. Her scarred lungs needed to download the code and get with the program. Now would be good, but she'd take later if she could get it.

Shuffling closer to the headstone, Ivy braved a full breath.

Damp air pushed into her lungs.

Her chest expanded. Pain burned behind her breastbone.

Tears pricked the corners of her eyes as she stared at the inscription. The words wavered, blurring in the gloom. She blinked, trying to hold onto the names, to recall their faces, sounding like a three pack a day smoker.

A thin wheeze escaped her.

She squeezed her eyes closed.

What a sham. Twenty-six years old and already halfway to being in the ground. Six feet under, toes cocked up, nothing but a cold corpse on an even colder slab. Death would be easier. A heck of a lot simpler too, but she couldn't do it. Couldn't give in. Couldn't give up. Couldn't listen to her doctors and stay indoors. Not anymore. Not after what her boss had done.

Gritting her teeth, Ivy fought through the pain.

Goddam Adam Worth.

She wanted to turn around, go home and kill him for setting her up. A lovely thought, but right now, the whole need-to-breathe thing took precedence. She couldn't wait much longer. The telltale signs were knocking on her mental door: the wheeze and claw of too little air, the awful ache in her chest, the persistent cough as cold Aberdeen air brutalized her lungs.

One shallow breath turned into two. And then another.

No good. It was *no good*. Her body refused to co-operate.

With a muffled curse, Ivy reached into her coat pocket.

Chilled plastic brushed her palm.

She hesitated a second, each breath fast and choppy, fingers curled around the medicine, not wanting to use it, but denial wasn't a girl's best friend. Neither was delaying. No matter how much she wanted to ignore reality, she couldn't. If she wanted to keep on keeping on, she needed a shot from her asthma inhaler. A crying shame. A real problem considering she didn't have any refills. She needed to ration her supply, but with the way things were going, she'd run out long before she found a computer, hacked the system, and proved Adam Worth was the traitor, not her.

Putting the inhaler from her pocket, she shook the small canister. The metal beads inside clacked, echoing though the quiet and across the cemetery, moving though tall, moss-covered headstones. Resignation settling like a stone in her stomach, Ivy lifted the inhaler. She took a hit. Vapor hissed from the plastic and into her mouth.

She breathed deep.

Wind gusts pushed at the treetops, rustling dead leaves, shoving at the branches above her head. Listening to the soft creak, Ivy waited. One Mississippi. Two Mississippi. Three—

The medicine went to work.

Her discomfort downgraded.

Her lungs filled with fresh air.

Exhaling hard, she inhaled again and tipped her head back. Pinpoint stars played peekaboo behind skeletal branches and thick clouds, obscuring her view of the night sky. Kind of fitting, all those clouds. A cover-up, mother nature's best, the sort one never saw coming until it was too late and the rain came down.

A metaphor for her life.

With a huff, she marveled at her own stupidity. An ethical hacker gone rogue. A homegrown terrorist—the label the US government had slapped on her over a week ago. All thanks to her boss, her friend and mentor, the guy responsible for recruiting her. The guy she'd trusted. The guy she'd thought walked on water after taking a position at INP Securities. Two years, fifteen days and seven hours at her dream job, hacking cyber systems, testing computer security and firewalls protecting classified files for the US government.

But that was ancient history.

Eleven days of disillusionment ago.

All while she struggled to come to terms with the fact Worth set her up. Had tied the noose, framing her so well she was now one of the FBIs most wanted.

"The jerk. The greedy, self-serving bastard." Ivy scowled at the headstone standing tall in front of her. A second passed. She smoothed her expression. Dead for over twenty years, her parents didn't deserve her anger. She wanted to say sorry instead, to apologize for not visiting sooner. For allowing years to lapse and the ocean separating them to get in the way.

"I'm sorry," she whispered, reaching out to pull the twisted vines away from the granite base. "I should have come sooner. Visited every chance I got. Aunt Violet would've let me, but..."

She trailed off, not knowing what to say. Or how to make amends.

Surrounded by death and the chill of midnight,

she fought the growing tide of tears, knowing she no longer owned the right to cry. Instead, she shuffled closer to the grave. Something sharp poked at her knee. Shifting to one side, she grabbed the offending stick and tossed it away. Damp earth soaked through her jeans as she continued to work.

Pace steady, she cleared the debris from the grave. Stone scraped over her skin, making her fingertips sting almost as much as her heart. Twenty years was a long time to stay away. To avoid the truth, but...

Ivy huffed. Life had a way of keeping people apart and making years speed by. No rhyme. No reason. Just a thick sense of loss that sank into her marrow. Now she didn't remember the place of her birth, much less the traditions that held the land.

Her throat tightened at the realization.

Swallowing around the lump, she grabbed at another vine. Slick with rain, the thick stock slid against her palms as she glanced up at the figure standing guard over her parents' grave. Unimpressed by her efforts, the angel glared at her, feathered wings spread, stone face smooth, expression unforgiving. The bold script forming her parents' names echoed the sentiment, carved letters throwing silent accusation like shovelfuls of dirt on top of a coffin.

"I know. I know," she murmured, accepting the censure, feeling the weight settle heavy on her shoulders. "But I'm here now, and I need help."

Raising her hand, Ivy traced her father's name. *Alistair MacPherson*. She didn't remember his face. Not really. Just shadowy features drawn from a six year old's memory, but it didn't matter. Even half a world away in America, she'd felt her dad's presence. Now wasn't any different. Time and place meant nothing. Somehow she knew he was listening. That tonight of all nights, heaven was real, and her dad was looking down on her, willing her to make it right. Hold steady, aim true and place the blame like a bulls-eye over her ex-boss's heart. "Tell me what to do. Where do I go from here? How do I make the authorities listen?"

Even as the question left her mouth, Ivy acknowledged the idiocy of it. She didn't need to ask. She knew what to do. And how to get Worth. The liar. The cheat. The poor excuse for a human being for stealing classified documents to sell to the highest bidder. But first, she needed to stay ahead of the task force, find a safe place to hide and—

"Ivy Macpherson, FBI—freeze!" The harsh voice echoed through the quiet.

"Scotland Yard!" a second man yelled at the same time, thick accent rising on a gust of wind. "Donnae move!"

Surprise made her jerk.

Panic sent her reeling.

She popped to her feet.

Her back to the agents, she tensed, muscles primed, heart thumping, her thoughts a scrambled mess inside her head. Time slowed. The vegetation and tombstones blurred as her mind sharpened. Shit. Shit, shit, *shit*! What to do? What should she do? Well, other than call herself a hundred different kinds of fool. She should never have come here. Should never have crossed the Atlantic. South America would've been a better bet. Coming home, reliving the past had been a miscalculation. A terrible, stupid mistake. By retracing her roots, she'd given the Feds a way to track her, a target to shoot for, the means to find her.

Not making any sudden moves, Ivy glanced over her shoulder. The moon peaked out from behind the clouds. Movement flashed in her periphery and...

bingo. Two men at six o'clock, one hundred feet away, give or take. Guns raised, the pair skirted the hedge, coming closer by the second.

Crap on a crumpet, how stupid could one person be?

The question spun through her mind. The answer sailed in without any prompting—fatally stupid, obviously. Proof positive approached from the other side of the clearing.

Which meant she needed a plan.

Right now.

Before the duo reached her, so...

Fight or flight? Make a run for it or stand and face men who would never listen? She knew it deep down. The truth wasn't something she could change. The FBI wasn't interested in her version of events. She'd tried that already. Had spent over an hour at INP headquarters answering questions before realizing the futility and escaping out a bathroom window.

Special Agent-in-charge Strickland had already made up his mind. Trying to convince him she'd been framed was like talking to a tank, one at full throttle, hoping it would change direction at the last minute. It would never happen. And she wouldn't survive federal custody. Adam Worth was just that good. Which meant she couldn't let them take her.

Not now.

Not a week from now.

She needed time. Enough to prove Worth's guilt. Enough to make things right.

The realization punched through. Adrenaline hit full force, rushing through her veins as Ivy scanned the shadows. Options. Escape routes. She needed both, and fast. Her gaze skipped over tall tombstones and slid between huge oaks. Recalling a map of the cemetery, Ivy held it in her mind's eye and turned to face her pursuers. She retreated a step. Ice and old leaves crackled beneath her boot treads. She didn't stop, moving away a little at a time.

A soft curse broke through the quiet.

The click of a gun being cocked followed. "Donnae do it, Macpherson. One false move, and I'll blow yer fool head off."

Raising her hands, she held them high, feigning surrender. Her gaze met Agent Strickland's, then jumped to the Scot. The burly cop leveled his weapon and, moving on silent feet, walked through a break in the hedgerow.

Swallowing, Ivy worked moisture into her mouth. "Hold up a second, Strickland. Let me explain. I was set up. If you'll just—"

"Don't move." The tail of his dark jacket fanning out behind him, Agent Strickland sidestepped between two headstones, correcting his line of sight.

Desperation set in. "I didn't do it." "I don't care."

"Of course, you do," she said, feeling the air thin as her panic sat on her chest. "You're FBI, for God's sake. You want the bad guy, not the person the bad guy set up. If you give me a chance, I can prove I'm—"

"Stay where you are."

"Innocent," she said, trying to reason with two guys holding guns on her.

Why she bothered, Ivy didn't know. No way would either of them believe her.

Worth had done a good job and covered his tracks.

She'd done the rest, hacking into the NSA database to exploit its weakness. Did it matter that she'd been given the green light by her boss? Or that she'd held the operational go-ahead form (signed by Worth) stating the mission parameters in her hands? No. Not even a little. It didn't matter that she'd done her job testing security levels or that she'd patched the hole in the firewall before retreating from the system. None of it mattered without proof—of which there was none.

At least, that's what everyone believed. What Worth was counting on too.

Ivy knew better.

Cyberspace existed outside the norms, on a different plane. Nothing ever truly got erased. Somewhere the proof of Worth's double dealing—along with the deleted mission file—lay hidden, just waiting for her to find it. In a single line of computer code maybe. In all those lovely lines of ones and zeros. Tucked away in places no one but the best hackers in the world knew existed. The dark net, her domain, a place she navigated better than most people did their hometown. A terrific skill set given present circumstances, but less than useless if she never got the chance to unleash it.

"Please, listen to me." Her gaze ping-ponged between the agents. The pair moved closer. Ivy walked backwards, keeping even distance between them. "Give me a computer and a little time. I know I can—"

A wall of heat hit her from behind.

Her skin prickled in warning.

Hands still in the air, Ivy glanced over her shoulder. Nothing. No fire. No vehicle throwing off heat. Just a cold, empty graveyard lit by weak moonlight.

The two agents moved closer.

"Crap," she muttered, retreating a step at a time. "I am so dead."

"Nay, lovely. Not yet." The voice, full of gravel, ghosted over her shoulder.

With a shriek, Ivy jumped forward, away from the threat.

A strong arm shot around her, yanked her backward and held on, locking her in a cage of hard muscle. Inferno-like heat bled from the stranger's body, obliterating her chill and...

Damn Agent Strickland.

The guy was nothing if not smart.

He'd sent another agent around to flank her. Now, she was caught. Trapped in a snare of her own making. She should have realized. She should have turned and run. Taken her chances with flying bullets and sprinted toward the cemetery's north wall. And now... she should be fighting, trying to break the guy's hold.

The realization kicked her brain into gear.

With a violent twist, she kicked backward. Her heel slammed into her captor's shin.

He cursed.

She bared her teeth, raised her foot a second time and—

*Wham!* She nailed him again.

"Fuck!"

The explicative exploded from his mouth. Warm breath rushed against her ear. A second arm joined the first, banding around her ribcage, compressing her chest, pumping more fear through her veins. He lifted her feet off the ground. Ivy flailed, knees pumping, feet flying, desperate to hit any part of him she could reach. She needed to get away. Right now. Before the other agents reached her. Before the guy holding her prisoner handed her over. Before her lungs shutdown and the asthma won, stealing her strength along with all her air.

Baring her teeth, Ivy raked him with her fingernails. "Let me go!"

"Bloody hell," he muttered, thick Scottish accent full of exasperation. He tightened his grip. The lockdown compressed her lungs. Black spots swam in her vision. She sucked in a desperate breath. An awful, familiar weight pressed down on her chest. Pain spiraled around her torso. With a curse, he adjusted his hold, lessened the pressure, and glanced down at her. His gaze met hers. "'Tis all right. Settle down. Breathe, lovely. I mean you no harm."

*Settle down? Breathe.* Just like that.

So simple. No need to worry. Leave all her cares behind. Ivy snarled at him. Was he insane? A few brain cells shy of a full load or something?

He planned to hand her over to the FBI, so no...the whole *no harm* assertion didn't fly. Neither did his gentle grip. Which was...odd. Yes, he'd immobilized her, but only enough to keep her from escaping. She wouldn't have bruises or feel the aftereffects in the morning. And yet, she knew better than to trust him.

It wasn't all right.

It hadn't been in Washington. And it wasn't now.

The guy holding her wasn't safe.

Intuition told her so. The heat in his eyes did the rest, making her renew the fight. She threw her head back. He lifted his chin, avoiding the blow and squeezed a little harder. She hissed at him. He reached around, grabbed her chin, and forced her head back. Dark purple eyes trapped hers and started to glow. A sinking sensation set in. The draw-and-pull tugged at her tension. Her skin prickled. Her heartbeat slowed and her limbs grew heavy.

Ivy blinked, struggling to stay with the fight. Peace shoved the intention aside. A lovely sense of safety invaded, washing through her and...hmm. That was nice, and God, he was incredibly warm. Really beautiful and—

He murmured to her.

Sluggishness hit. Her eyes drifted closed. She forced both back open, then shook her head to clear her mind.

Something was off. The guy holding her was all wrong. Him and his gorgeous face and dark hair and mesmerizing eyes and—she should be doing something. She frowned. Shouldn't she? The thought circled. Ivy nodded. Yes, absolutely. Action of some sort was required. But as she stared at him, she lost track of the plan. Questions and concerns drifted away, making her want to fall into him and go to sleep.

Maybe that was it.

Maybe she was dreaming. Maybe he wasn't really here and the glow in eyes wasn't real, but...

Raising her hand, she grabbed his biceps.

Leather creaked beneath her palm. Hard muscle met her touch. Huh. He felt solid, like sinew and bone, not part of her imagination. The way he held her, the warmth he radiated, the way he looked at her: all of it seemed *real*. Not something she'd invented.

"Who are you?"

"Tydrin."

"A cop?"

"Nay, not police." His voice deepened into something dark. Something dangerous. Something she couldn't resist. "Trust me, Ivy. I'll keep you safe."

The shimmer in his eyes intensified.

Tingles burst across the nape of her neck, then slithered down her spine. Her brain went fuzzy. Thoughts slipped away. Ivy fought the mental slide. *Struggle. Don't give up.* She needed to get away. A false hope born of true desperation. She couldn't escape. Was caught fast, unable to move. The longer he looked at her, the worse it became. Her muscles loosened, drawing her toward relaxation. Ivy went limp in his arms. He studied her a moment, then hummed in approval. She opened her mouth to protest. No sound came out.

Strickland yelled something.

The Scottish agent answered, voice barely penetrating the fog clouding her mind.

Oh, she heard the words. The meaning simply didn't register.

The FBI didn't matter anymore. Neither did the danger the agents presented. All that mattered was *him,* the mystery man with shimmering eyes. She couldn't avoid the glow. Couldn't tear her gaze away or protest when he turned her in his arms.

With a quick dip, he picked her up, cradling her against his chest, and one last thought registered. Something was wrong. Seriously *wrong* with him. Eyes weren't supposed to shimmer like that, and as his mouth curved and he murmured "There's a good lass." before turning his attention to the agents, Ivy knew nothing would ever be the same.

Least of all her.

# 3

T O KILL or not to kill. That was the question.
Gaze locked on the FBI agent, Tydrin debated a moment. It wouldn't take much. A flick of his fingers. A little swirl, a lot of arm action combined with a burst of magic and...poof gone. Fireball central and two dead agents, nothing but human ash spread over the cruel lines of a desolate cemetery. Kind of fitting, actually. Way too tempting, but well... shite. He couldn't do it. Not with the lass in his arms and his dragon half in full protection mode.

Ivy needed help, not added trouble.

And a couple of dead agents? Tydrin pursed his lips. Aye. For sure. Not the best way to get on the lass's good side.

Under his influence, soothed by his magic, he cradled the female closer. She sighed and settled in, curling up like a well-fed kitten in his arms. The underside of his chin brushed the top of her head. Her long damp hair clung to his skin, getting caught in old day stubble. He rubbed his mouth over the soft strands. A sense of peace invaded him body, mind and heart. His muscles loosened, releasing some of the tension.

He exhaled in relief, relaxing under her influence and...hmm, she was sweet. So alluring with her dark red hair and pale, freckled skin. Far too pretty to be a fugitive. Hunted. Trapped. Wanted by the FBI.

Way too vulnerable without him to protect her.

Cloaked by a powerful spell, Tydrin made up his mind. He retreated, backing away from the agents toward the copse of evergreens. His boot treads crunched over the gravel path. A long- limbed oak creaked above his head. He shut down all sound, silencing the echo, and disappeared into the fog of invisibility. Both humans cursed, then split, moving in different directions, sweeping the area, determined to pick up Ivy's trail. He snorted. Winter air attacked his breath, streaming into puffs in front of his face. He ignored the frosty swirl and narrowed his focus.

No chance in hell.

The pair would never find her. Not with his magic up and running.

He watched anyway, eyes trained on the threat, unwilling to lower his guard. Rightly so. The impenetrable shield he conjured was required. Necessary even. Practically a biological imperative. He carried precious cargo, a female so rare—so precious—his dragon half tuned in without prompting, monitoring her bio-energy, seeking her comfort, ensuring she remained foggy and free of fear.

Regret hit him like an upper cut.

He almost balked.

Almost backed off.

Almost reconsidered his plan, put her down, and walked away.

*Almost,* but not quite.

He couldn't do it. Which made him a first-rate fool. A bastard of epic proportions for placing his needs before hers, but...shite. His dragon half refused to let her go. Not until he got what he craved—a taste of her energy, and more time with her. More conversation. A helluva lot more closeness too. The kind that would see her skin pressed against his.

Unaware of her peril, Ivy snuggled in, absorbed his warmth, trusting him to keep his word and her safe. His conscience squawked, shaking a bony finger at him. Clenching his teeth, Tydrin swallowed a growl.

Great. Just wonderful. As if he needed the reminder.

He knew it was wrong. Felt the truth of it settle deep inside him, in the place where right battled unjust and impulse challenged self-control. He had no right to hold her. Shouldn't have used magic to muddle her mind either. The move was pure jackass. A method honorable males refused to use.

Not that his fall from grace mattered.

He'd blown his chance at being *honorable* years ago.

Recall pressed mental buttons inside his head. Memory flamed. Guilt blew sky-high. The quick spike of his temper followed. He glanced down at the female in his arms. Eyes closed, body lax and cheek pressed to his shoulder, she floated in the mind-fog he'd created for her.

Tydrin's throat went tight.

Bloody hell. *Ivy MacPherson.* Of all the miserable luck. What a terrible turn of events. God forgive him for his foolishness. He wished he could go back and fix it. Needed to rewind the clock. Wanted to make it right now more than ever. Too bad time didn't work that way. No matter how much he wanted to, he couldn't rewrite history or pretend it hadn't happened.

Oh, he'd tried—for years...and years.

Ivy brought it rushing back in an instant. His loss of control. The fireball's awful flight as it went astray. The explosion, the burning house, the smell of charred flesh and mangled bodies. His fault. His mistake. His cross to bear alone. At least, he'd thought so...

Until tonight.

Now he realized it wasn't true. He wasn't alone. Ivy lived the same hell every day. Aye, he might carry the guilt, but she lived with the pain. Different views of the same moment in time, the same abiding sense of loss.

With a curse, Tydrin stepped around the edge of the evergreens. He needed to head back to Cairngorm. Shift into dragon form. Get airborne. Fly to safety before the cops called in reinforcements, dragged out their thermal imaging equipment, and got a bead on his heat signature. A distant, yet distinct possibility, but never mind that. He had a bigger problem on the horizon—Ivy.

The lass wouldn't stay compliant long.

High-energy females never did. Their minds were too strong to be fogged by magic for more than a few minutes. A strong breed, HEs recovered quickly and retaliated even faster. So aye, better to move now and worry about her reaction later...when he landed inside his mountain home. Had her miles from anything or anyone.

Safely hidden from the humans hunting her.

Glancing over his shoulder, Tydrin checked on the agents' progress. Guns pointing toward the ground, confused looks on their faces, the men circled the spot where she'd disappeared. The pair glanced around. One went right. The other turned left, searching for Ivy behind tombstones and along the tree lined path. Their boots crunched over gravel.

Tydrin snorted. "Good luck finding us, lads."

"What?"

He glanced down.

Ivy blinked, looking up at him with sleepy eyes.

His mouth curved. Man, she was sweet. So soft and warm. So adorably incoherent. So delicious with the powerful pulse of bio-energy outlining her slight frame. The blue light of her aura mesmerized him for a moment. She licked her bottom lip. Desire curled in the pit of his stomach, then exploded, rushing through his veins, weakening his knees, making him want so hard he lost all sense of himself. Right. Wrong. Neither mattered as his body reacted, tightening around her.

She squirmed in his arms.

He gentled his hold as duty shoved lust aside.

Tydrin sucked in a breath. What did he think he was doing? He needed to remember who she was, and his crime. He shouldn't want her. Not like this. No way he deserved to know her, never mind touch her. Accident or nay, he'd killed her kin, destroyed her life, forced her from the safety of her childhood home.

An ache expanded behind his breastbone.

Ivy squinted up at him.

He stared back, an apology on the tip of his tongue. He should come clean. Tell her who and what he was, then set her down and distract the authorities long enough for her to escape.

It was the proper thing to do.

"Hello, lovely," he said instead. Feeling like an idiot, unable to look away, he held her gaze. "You've come back tae me then, have ye?"

She frowned. "Where'd I go?"

"Away for a minute or two."

"Guess I'm back now."

"Appears so."

Studying him like an insect under a microscope, she pursed her lips.

Ravenous hunger killed reason, then went rogue, urging him to dip his head, take her mouth, and... bloody hell. Talk about a bad idea. One taste would never be enough. She was so pretty. Too striking. The picture of perfection with her messy auburn hair and sapphire blue eyes.

Plugged into her energy, he felt her mind sharpen. Her eyes grew dark with temper. The glow surrounding her deepened, then burned, making his dragon purr in pleasure. Tydrin hummed in reaction, the burn of her bio-energy taunting him and...oh, baby. She was too good, so powerful he couldn't stop himself.

He dipped his head.

His mouth brushed over hers. "Hey!"

"Let me." Drunk on her taste, he nipped her bottom lip. Glory-glory-hallelujah. He'd found his new calling—kissing her every minute of every day. Christ, she tasted good, like dark chocolate and spiced wine. "Just a taste, lass...tae tide me over."

Raising her hand, she planted her palm on his jaw and shoved his face away. "Get over yourself and away from me, mister. Otherwise, I'll—"

"What? What will ye do, lass?" With a playful flick, he tasted the corner of her mouth. She sucked in a sharp breath. Lifting his head, he raised a brow. "Hit me?"

"I've got an awesome right cross."

He grinned. "I've no doubt, but here's something tae consider."

She coughed, the rasp sounding wheezy, and scowled at him. "Enlighten me."

He jostled her, making her aware of where she sat. "You've still got the FBI tae avoid."

"Shit. Put me down." Alarm sparked in her eyes. She twisted in his arms, struggling to see over his shoulder. "How close are they?"

"Not very," he said, watching her reaction, hating her fear. "They've gone the other way."

"Thank God."

"Aye. Or you could simply thank me."

"For what?"

"For saving your fine arse."

She opened her mouth, no doubt to blast him for his comment.

He cut her off. "Relax, lass. 'Tisn't anything but a bit of teasing. You're safe."

"Safe." A death grip on his coat, she whispered the word as though she'd forgotten its meaning.

"Aye."

Her gaze raked his face. "You don't look safe."

He huffed. Smart lass. With his hunger gone nuclear, she'd hit the nail on its head. He wasn't safe. Not even close. Quite the opposite in fact. Lucky for her, he prided himself on self-control. On a female being willing as well. "I'm safe enough, lovely."

"You really need to put me down."

Moonlight pieced through the clouds. Tydrin shook his head. "Not until I'm ready."

"You can't just—"

"I can, Ivy." He met her gaze, daring her to contradict him. "Fight me or nay, it willnae matter.

I mean tae have my way, so you need tae decide."

"On what?"

"How you want it tae go?"

Her brows popped skyward. "I have a choice?"

He chuckled. Christ, she delighted him. Aye, he liked the look of her. No question. She was a beautiful female. But her mind—her sharp intellect, surly temper, and quick wit? Shite. He suspected, given time, he'd like those things about her best of all.

"You always have a choice, lass. Cooperate or nay. Accept my protection or be captured by the police. 'Tis for you tae decide."

"For you to decide," she repeated, throwing him a disgruntled look. "Famous last words."

"Could be," he murmured, teasing her a little before turning serious once more. "But I promise you one thing, Ivy. You've a safe place with me. The FBI and Scotland Yard will never find you. You'll have time and more tae find the proof you need."

Worry darkened her expression. "At what price, Tydrin?"

Pleased she remembered his name, he smiled. "An open mind and your time, lovely. Naught more, no less."

"And sex?"

Surprise made him blink. Well, hell. Of all the things he expected her to say, that hadn't been one of them. An image of her in his bed rose in his mind— long hair loose, pale skin on display, her legs spread in invitation. His body jumped at the idea, hardening him in an instant. "I willnae say no, as long as you ask nicely."

She snorted, the sound half-amused, half-disgusted. "Dream on, buddy. I'm only asking so we're clear. Friends, that's it. No expectations beyond that."

*Friends?* Shite, that wasn't going to go well. Especially since he wanted her naked and underneath him. And half hoped she would be by morning. "I willnae expect or force it, but know right now, Ivy...I want you."

"It's why you intervened, the reason you're helping me." "Aye."

His honesty worried her.

He could see the wariness in her eyes. And yet, she didn't panic. She studied him instead, expression serious, mind identifying all the angles. Entranced, Tydrin watched her. He could practically see her thinking. Felt her mental wheels turning. Sensed her intellect flip through the intricacies—accept or abandon the possibilities—as she tried to decide. Play it safe and try to escape him. Or be brave, take him at his word, and trust him.

*Be brave*, he wanted to say.

Patience stopped him.

She needed to make up her own mind. He refused to rush her. Time was the only thing he could truly give her.

He wanted her too much to allow the separation. No way could he set her down and watch her walk away. Not now. In just moments, he'd doubled down, become invested in seeing where she would lead him — in getting to know her, in helping her, in keeping her safe...and showing her the truth of his race.

Why he needed her to acknowledge him—and Dragonkind—he didn't know. Call it foolhardy. Chalk it up to a need for acceptance. Or mayhap the chance to undo a mistake. Whatever. The reason didn't matter. She was here. So was he. Labeling the need wouldn't make it go away, so...screw it. He was jumping in, diving down and digging in.

Tearing her gaze from his, Ivy scanned the shadows between old oaks. "Is Agent Strickland really gone?"

"Cross my heart, hope tae—"

"Die?" she asked, a hopeful note in her voice.

He laughed. "Feisty wee baggage, arenae ye?"

"Believe it," she said. "And you can put me down. I won't run."

"I'll have your word first, lass."

"I'll have access to a computer?"

"Any one you want."

"And a roof over my head?"

"Safest one in all of Scotland."

She drew a breath. The inhale made her cough. One hand pressed to her chest, she suppressed the rasp and nodded. "Okay."

"Promise?"

"Yes." Her chin firmed, then leveled. "And when I make a promise, Tydrin, I never break it."

"Good enough. Now..." Watching her closely, he let the pause expand, warning her. Quick on the up-take, she froze against him, waiting for the punch line. Had he said smart? Well, call her brilliant and be done with it. She didn't miss a beat. Or any of the nuances. "I'm going tae need you tae keep your promise tae be open-minded."

Ivy threw him a questioning look.

Releasing her legs, he dropped her feet to the ground. "Things are about tae get a wee bit strange for you."

Standing in the circle of his arms, she shifted, seeking separation.

He tightened his hold, refusing to release her even as regret rose. He didn't want to scare her, but explaining wouldn't work. Actions spoke louder than words. Ivy needed to see to believe. So instead of warning her, he unleashed his magic.

Wind gusts blew between the tombstones.

Heat exploded around them.

In a panic, Ivy pushed against his chest.

Tydrin called on his dragon and shifted. Frigid night air spilled over his black, purple-tipped scales. Frozen earth pushed between his talons, covering the tips of his razor-sharp claws. Ivy inhaled hard. Tydrin didn't give her the chance to scream. Holding the lass in the palm of his paw, he unfurled his wings and leapt skyward, into the unforgiving light of the moon.

## 4

S NOWFLAKES SWIRLED over her head as the
world went topsy-turvy. Ivy squeezed her eyes
shut. She needed a moment to acclimatize. Just
a few seconds. A minute at most to figure it out and
come up with a plan. After that, she'd know exactly
how to—

The dragon banked right, angling into a tight turn.

G-force velocity picked her up.

Time slowed.

Gravity shifted.

She hung weightless a moment, suspended above
the cradle of his paw before the laws of relativity took
hold. She stopped going up and started to come down.
Her shoulder landed in the center of his palm an instant before her hip hit. The impact made her gasp.
The slip-and-slide made her cling to one of his talons
to keep from falling. The wind whistled between his
claws. Smooth interlocking dragon skin brushed her
cheek.

Her brain scrambled.

This wasn't happening. It couldn't be real. She
wasn't here. He hadn't transformed, gone from man to
dragon without warning. Wasn't holding her captive

or...holy crap. Dreaming. She must be *dreaming*. Lost consciousness somewhere along the way. Or be stuck in between, suffering from lack of oxygen with her lungs in lockdown.

The explanation made sense. Accounted for the nightmare scenario, and the fact she'd left nice-and-normal behind to fly solo into the realm of fiction.

Ivy swallowed past the lump in her throat. Yes. Absolutely. A dream qualified as an excellent reason for the hallucination. Was a solid contender in a world gone topsy-turvy—inexplicably, undeniably crazy. Any second now, she'd wake up, open her eyes, feel the soft cotton comforter against her face.

Frigid wind burned over her skin

*Wake up. Wake up. WAKE UP!*

Paralyzed by fear, the words echoed inside her head.

Ivy forced her eyes open.

City lights blurred into streaks below her. Snow turned to rain, pelting her jacket before saturating her skin. Water rolled down her cheek. A shiver rattled through her and...oh, God. Not good. The raindrops felt real—skin chilling, hair tangling, jean soaking genuine. Unable to get enough air, Ivy started to pant. Frigging hell. A minute wasn't going to be long enough. An hour wouldn't be either. Give her a year to mull it over and the situation still wouldn't make sense.

She was flying. *Flying*—at break neck speed high above the city of Aberdeen.

Dark wings spread wide, the dragon dipped beneath a thick storm cloud. Her vision blurred. She forced it back into focus. The landscape came into view. Damp, narrow streets snaked between small houses with smoking chimneys. Tiled roofs gave away to large trees and a walled garden asleep beneath winter's watchful eye.

Recall provided a quick snapshot.

Such a lovely little spot. So charming at dusk. Or so she'd thought while walking past it on her way to the cemetery. From a half a mile up, however, everything, including her perspective, changed. None of it seemed the least bit delightful now.

The dragon dove into another harrowing turn.

Velocity pressed her deeper into his palm.

Ivy opened her mouth to scream. Cold air invaded her throat, stalling the breath in her lungs. Her chest compressed. The shriek died in her throat. A wheeze clawed its way out instead as pain drove spikes through her breastbone. Her vision dimmed as oxygen deprivation set in, scattering her thoughts like bowling pins.

Clinging to sanity, Ivy narrowed her focus. *Think.* She needed to think, but even as self-preservation surfaced, the air thinned. Soon it would disappear, and she'd be in serious trouble. Wouldn't stand a chance when her asthma kicked in, took over, shut down her ability to function. The tide would rise, and she'd be swept away, engulfed in a medical crisis, unable to stop what happened next.

Panic shoved fear out of the way, hitting her with adrenaline. Her muscles tightened as the blood rush stuck like a shot of epinephrine. Locked in a spasm, her lungs opened enough for her to take a shallow breath. The infuse of oxygen went straight to her head, and...thank God. Her brain was back, dragging a healthy dose of fight with it.

Wedging her hands between her chest and the beast's claw, she pushed. Warm scales pressed against her palms. Goosebumps spread on her skin. Baring her teeth, she kept shoving.

No good.

Zero movement.

Not an ounce of give.

She tried again. His talons flexed. Razor-sharp claws inched closer to her face. Ivy froze. He relaxed his grip. She stayed still, heart pumping, mind churning to formulate a viable plan. She needed one —right now, but...what was she supposed to do? What would work? How could she win against a dragon?

Breathing in painful bursts, she stared up at it.

Or rather, him.

Calling the beast currently kidnapping her a *him* seemed like a good idea. Particularly since clinging to hope she sat in the middle of a dream wasn't working. No matter how much she wanted to deny it, she couldn't. Not anymore. He was here. So was she. Which meant...

The guy with the gorgeous eyes and libido-stoking voice had turned into a dragon. A holy-crap-just-kill-me-now *dragon*.

One with jagged horns on his head. Although, why that concerned her most she didn't know. Maybe she was an idiot. Ivy frowned. Yes, definitely an idiot, considering the horns should be the least of her worries. Other things took precedence. The huge fangs in his mouth raised serious warning flags. The giant wings and the brutal lash of his bared tail topped her list as well. The talons tipped by long wicked-looking claws, though, ranked as the most important. More of a threat. The biggest problem. With good reason too.

Ivy eyed the sharp tips inches from her head.

A sound of distress left her throat. The pitiful croak barely registered. Was such a weak attempt at screaming the dragon didn't hear her. Or notice how much she struggled to breathe.

Ivy willed air into her lungs. Nothing happened. Panic erupted, closing her airway faster than usual. No...just no. She knew better than to let fear shut her down. Had learned early in life she she needed to stay calm. Must focus, remain centered and concentrate. Otherwise the asthma would win. Take over a little at a time. Steal her air and then her life.

Battling to stay conscious, Ivy fought to draw another breath. Frigid air washed over her teeth. She coughed. The hacking sound drifted between the dragon's claws as he leveled off over a river. Moonlight glinted off rippling waves. Cargo boats bobbed against the concrete pier, silent and stern in the water as her windpipe contracted. Light-headedness swamped her. The lights along the dock edge blurred into jagged streaks. Her brain sloshed inside her skull, crippling reason as desperation took hold. Curling her hand into a fist, she punched the top of his talon.

The feeble attempt caught his attention.

Tucking his chin, he glanced down at her. Shimmering purple eyes met hers. "All right, lovely?"

The question drifted on a voice she recognized. Tydrin. Of course. It couldn't be anyone other than him, Mr. Tall-Dark-and-Dangerous, her guardian angel in the cemetery turned monster in dark of night.

Floating inside her own head, Ivy tried to laugh. No sound came out, but...wow. It was almost funny— the circumstances, him saving her only to kill her in the end.

"Tydrin."

"Talk to me, luv."

Almost out of air, she shook her head. He frowned. She twisted in his paw, and with one last burst of energy, reached for her coat pocket. Her inhaler. She must reach her medicine. Right now. Before she passed out, and it became too late.

"I'm sorry for frightening you, but..." Concern salted his tone. The velocity of his flight slowed as he nudged her with his talon. "Ivy?"

Agony tightened its grip. "C-can't breathe. Asthma. N-need...my..."

Fumbling in her pocket, she fought to finish her sentence. To make him understand. To ask for help. But it was too late. Her chest heaved as all the oxygen disappeared, deflating her lungs, stealing her hope, slowing her heart.

Ivy listened to the sluggish beat, knowing it would be the last time she heard it.

Dead and gone.

Cold and grey.

Nothing but a corpse in a dragon's paw.

Tears trickled from the corners of her eyes. She smiled through her anguish. It was strange and somehow appropriate. Only fitting that she die in Scotland, the place of her birth, in a country so old myth it overcame reality, allowing the beat of dragon wings to carry her into the afterlife.

Hollow inside, she went limp in his paw.

"Jesus Christ." The harsh curse came from far away, through a dim tunnel filled with pain. "Hang on, Ivy. I'm landing. I'll help you, just..."

Rising dark and melodic in her mind, his words floated away.

A black hole opened beneath her. Her world ceased spinning. Ivy let her eyes close and herself go, drifting into nothingness as the abyss grew teeth and swallowed her whole.

## 5

FEAR LIT A FIRE UNDER TYDRIN. He banked hard and increased his wing speed. Cold air streamed over the weave of his interlocking dragon skin. Gale force winds funneled, rattling the bladed spikes along his spine. The high rise closest to him groaned. Thick glass shook in steel window casings, killing the quiet. Dragon senses pinpoint sharp, he heard humans curse from behind the granite facade. Lights flipped on in the apartments closest to him.

Tydrin ignored the light show.

None of it mattered.

Fuck the collateral damage.

Human upheaval be damned. He'd fry the entire neighborhood—KO the entire block—to ensure Ivy's safety.

One eye on the skyline, he checked on her again.

Concern escalated into serious worry. The lass was in serious trouble. Barely breathing. Laying limp in his paw. So pale her skin appeared translucent in the moonlight. Oh so not good. Another minute, and she'd tumbled down the rabbit hole, straight into physical meltdown. Cardiac arrest wasn't an impossibility. Neither was brain damage from lack of oxygen.

The downward dip in her bio-energy told him so. The fact she panted, struggling to draw shallow breaths, filled in the blanks. He needed to fold his wings and land. Right now. The sooner he set down in the courtyard behind the Dragon's Horn—the pub he owned with the other warriors in his pack— and got his hands on her, the sooner she would stabilize. The skin-to-skin contact would help. His magic—opening a channel to the Meridian and treating her with a dose of healing energy— would do the rest.

He frowned. A least, he hoped so.

The plan would work—in theory. Reality, however, was far more pragmatic.

Feeding a female energy took great skill. It started with a meeting of the minds. Male to female. Dragonkind to human. A coupling which necessitated his dragon half's cooperation. By no means a given. Finicky by nature, his dragon must agree and accept the female as his own. A process his kind called energy-fuse and...shite. It was tricky as hell. Difficult to accomplish. Hard on the system if achieved. Dangerous if forced. The worst kind of unpredictable— the equivalent of hitting a moving target while flying backwards blindfolded.

Not impossible, but a far cry from easy either.

Hurtling around an ornate church steeple, Tydrin angled into the last turn and put on the brakes. His wing's black webbing shuddered in the blowback. His muscles shrieked in protest. Ignoring the discomfort, Tydrin hung suspended a moment, his focus on the walled courtyard below him. Streetlights painted golden swathes across the pub's slate roof. His eyes narrowed. X marked the spot. Right there. Ten feet from the back door. Less than a fifty foot drop to the ground. He exhaled hard. Sparks shot from his nostrils, lighting up the gloom as he folded his wings.

Gravity grabbed hold.

He dropped out of the sky.

Halfway down, he mined Ivy's bio-energy. Still shaky. Not improving and—

Her vital signs plummeted, reaching dangerous levels. Air rasped from her mouth. Her chest shuddered as her body spasmed.

She jerked inside his paw. Tydrin cursed.

*"Hold on, Ivy."* The words echoed inside his head. He pushed each one into hers, opening a line through mind-speak, praying his voice reached her. Reassured her. Helped calm her enough to draw more air. *"Just a bit longer, lovely. I'm almost there."*

His paws thumped down.

His talons curled under.

Cobblestone cracked, sending fissures out like spiderwebs as metal patio furniture jumped. The clang echoed off stone walls. Water sloshed over the lip of the oversized fountain. The trio of serpents sitting at its center—tails and heads entwined, fanged mouths in full hiss—listed to one side as Tydrin tucked his wings. The second the webbing met his sides, he shifted to human form and conjured a pair of sweat pants.

The switch caused Ivy to slump against his chest. Her head wobbled on her shoulders. His arms came around her. Holding her steady, he slipped his hand beneath her coat collar and cupped the nape of her neck. Bare skin met his. His palm heated as his magic engaged. Energy sparked. The Meridian surged, opening a channel deep inside him. A click sounded inside his head. His dragon half snarled and...

Tydrin hummed.

Oh aye. Just like that. Mission accomplished, connection complete.

He was powered up and plugged in. Deep inside the female's veins and...thank Christ and every single one of his angels. His dragon was on board and hooked in, accepting his will instead of fighting the fuse.

Good for him. Even better for Ivy.

The influx of energy would open her lungs and help her breathe. And while she fed— aligning her life force with his, taking what she needed from him— his dragon half would hunt for the cause. He must root out the problem in order to fix it. Heal whatever ailed her, then ensure she remained stable throughout her stay in Aberdeen.

he'd said something about asthma.

He'd start there, deep inside her lungs: seek the source, identify the underlying condition, remove the threat. Now that he'd connected, he knew he could help her. A little time. A lot of effort, and she'd be right as rain. Breathing again. Conscious once more. Back to herself instead of half dead in his arms.

But not yet.

She needed more. More of his skin against hers. A stronger connection to the Meridian. More of the healing energy he pumped into her veins.

Shoving her coat out of the way, he slid his hand beneath her shirt. His palm found the base of her spine. She twitched. Tydrin increased the pressure, spread his fingers wide, reaching as much of her as he could. Her chest rose and fell on a raspy breath. Dipping his head, he set his cheek to hers. His mouth drifted to her temple. He whispered her name, trying to wake her, willing her to accept more from him. She fought for a second, denying herself, hurting him before—

She turned her head toward him.

Her lips brushed his throat.

The connection amplified, bombarding him with sensation.

Prickles exploded down his spine. Ecstasy rushed through his veins, sensitizing his skin, brutalizing his senses, wrapping him in glorious, soul-ravishing warmth. Tydrin shuddered. Bloody hell. That felt good. Beautifully intense. Beyond all experience. Pleasure pushed the envelope, went supersonic and—

Sensation lashed him.

The pressure increased, driving him toward the edge of control. Overload threatened to shove him off track. His eyelashes flickered. Tydrin bore down, manipulating the flow of energy, feeding her the right amount, refusing to hurt her. The rush downgraded from brutal to magnificent. He groaned. Hmm, baby. She was amazing. So goddamn gorgeous as she took what he offered.

"There's my lass. Good girl." Drunk on delight, he murmured the praise against her skin.

Another wave of bliss hit him.

Tydrin swayed on his feet.

Closing his eyes, he narrowed his focus and sank into the powerful stream. His legs folded until his knees hit the ground. The fountain gurgled as the damp seeped through his jogging pants to touch his skin. Not that he cared. With his fire dragon in full throttle, the cold barely register. So instead of heading for the door—and his quarters underground, beneath the pub—he planted his arse on the ground and pulled Ivy into his lap. She settled like a gift, thighs draped over his, bottom pressed to his groin, face tucked beneath his chin.

Wrapped around her like a blanket, the world faded.

His dragon sighed, accepting her fully as his mind drifted, the connection filling him so full he knew he'd met his match. His mate. The female made and meant for him. In that moment, Tydrin forgot about the complications. Lost track of right. Pushed aside wrong. Left past wrongs where they lay, in the dirt where each one belonged. None of it mattered anymore. She was here, and he was ruined for anyone else.

"Take more, Ivy. Let me give you more."

She whispered his name.

He fed her more healing energy, overloading her system, narrowing his focus on her lungs. Right there, in the bottom half of both lobes. His magic cranked the dial, magnifying the problem. Now he could see what ailed her. Shite. So much scar tissue. Way too much pain. No wonder she was having trouble breathing, suffering in the worst possible way.

Concentrating on her malady, Tydrin opened the valve and upped the current. The Meridian pulsed. His dragon half regulated the flow, sending a continuous stream into her chest, pushing the equivalent of magical medicine into her lungs. Her aura started to glow. The bright blue light heated the air around him, then turned inward to repair the damage.

Air rushed into her lungs.

Her chest filled. Her ribcage expanded. One deep breath turned into another. And then another. Over and over. Again and again. How long he sat cradling her—minutes. Hours. The rest of night—he didn't know. Didn't care much either. Healing energy treatments took time. And he would make sure she ended the night one hundred percent healthy. Able to breathe without pain or the aid of an asthma inhaler ever again.

Unable to resist, he traced one of her eyebrows with his mouth. She stirred, shifting on his lap. Lifting his head, he jumped to her cheek, brushing soft kisses on her skin. "Ivy?"

Her eyelashes fluttered against his jaw. "What are you doing?"

"Helping you. Healing you."

"You're gonna regret that," she said, words slurred as she took more, losing herself in the glory of her first energy feeding. Rubbing her cheek against his, she slid her arms around him and hugged him close. Her fingertips played, drifting over his bare back. "I'm trouble."

"Are ye now?"

"Always have been."

Bullshite. His female might be challenging with her quick mind and stubborn nature, but she wasn't *trouble*. She was perfection personified. "Who told you that?"

"My aunt. FBI too."

"Idiots...every single one."

Ivy huffed, the sound full of amusement. Snuggling closer, she drew circles on his shoulder blades. Tydrin shivered as lust surged, merging with desperate need. "I feel better. Doesn't hurt anymore."

"Good." Raising her chin with his thumb, he tilted her head back. His gaze roamed over her face. Eyes closed, expression peaceful and body relaxed, she rested against him. His mouth curved. Fantastic. Not a care in the world. Exactly the way he wanted her. At least, until she healed. After that, there would be time and more to explain the bond he now shared with her... and that he would never let her go. "It'll feel even better come morning."

"Okay," she said, drifting toward exhaustion.

"Go tae sleep, Ivy."

"You'll stay?"

"Of course. You cannae get rid of me so easily." "We'll see."

Aye, they would. Sooner rather than later too.

Forget restraint. Throw away his original plan of a temporary tryst. Ivy might not know it yet, but he planned to keep her. Some slight of hand, a little trickery, a well-planned seduction, and she wouldn't know what hit her.

With a sigh of contentment, Tydrin listened to her breath and watched her fall asleep. Aye. No question. His approach was solid. Do it right, and she'd be his—bonded deep, so attached to him she'd never leave. Pressing a soft kiss to her brow, Tydrin nodded. Sound reasoning. Seemed like a plan. The best course of action, but for one thing...

Energy-fuse—the magical bond between mates—couldn't be forced.

Unlike him, Ivy had a choice.

Accept or deny him. Love or leave him.

With his dragon half fixated on her, Tydrin yearned for the first. He needed her to welcome his attention. Wanted to give her the world. Which left him with one recourse—spend the time, spoil her rotten, make her want to stay.

Or lose her forever.

## 6

I VY KNEW something was wrong the instant she woke up. She never went to bed in her clothes. Always took the time to change into an oversized t-shirt. A pair of roomy boxer shorts usually made the list labeled sleepwear too.

She shifted under the covers.

Denim rasped over her skin and...yeah. Definite reason for concern. Something was off. Forget about the jeans and wool sweater she wore. More reasons for worry popped up. The mattress was too soft, the shadowy outlines of bedposts too tall, the blankets too light and—

She stretched.

Her palm slid over something hard.

Still more asleep than awake, she frowned. What the heck was that? She didn't own a dog. Her cat—poor Fester, may he rest in peace—had died last year. And a boyfriend? Ivy huffed. Ha, right. No need to go there. Or revisit her inadequacies. But even as she told herself to leave it alone, the question circled—how would she ever land a man when she spent all her time holed up behind computer screens?

Great question.

Super observation.

No help at all.

Especially since her hand wasn't lying, 'cause... wow. That sure felt like a man's chest. Warm. Smooth. Muscular in all the right places. She let her hand wander lower and pursed her lips. Maybe not a chest. Maybe those were abs, the perfect contours of a kick-ass six pack.

With a hum, she trailed her fingers over the ridges, then up his side. Oh, nice. Wicked good. Long and strong. Rugged and ripped. Ivy sighed in contentment. Awesome. He was the best imaginary man she'd ever dreamed.

The thought made her smile.

Exhaustion made her snuggle in.

He grumbled in his sleep. The growl vibrated against her ear and...huh. The reverberation sounded real. A little too vocal for a dream. Swimming through the soupy mix of slumber, Ivy cracked her eyelids open. A wide shoulder came into view. She squinted at it. Beautiful. Such an incredible sight, although strange too considering she lay half on top of him, cheek pressed to his chest, hand snug against his side, one thigh wedged between both of his.

Warning bells rang inside her head.

The mind-fog thickened, drowning out the clang of unease. She yawned and let herself drift, enjoying the feel of strong arms around her. Nothing to worry about here. No need to sound the alarm. Everything was A-Okay. It must be. He was so warm, and she didn't want to move. Not yet. Maybe not ever.

She sighed. Terrific plan. She should definitely stay put. Take advantage, get some more rest, and float for a while. She never got to sleep in anymore. Her job didn't allow for it and...

So good.

He felt so damned good.

Lifting her head a fraction, Ivy let her gaze roam. Killer biceps...awesome. A ripped forearm...perfect. A huge hand curled around her much smaller one...you betcha.

She stared at the long fingers laced with hers a second.

The slumber-driven haze receded. Awareness surged as prickles slid over her shoulders and down her spine. The warm current played havoc with her focus, the message clear: *go back to sleep, lovely*. The endearment spiraled inside her head, tugged at her tension, tweaked a memory even as it tempted her to obey.

Ivy shook her head.

*Wake up! Concentrate.*

The command wavered between her temples. Ivy narrowed her focus, forcing herself to stay with it. She needed to figure out how the hell she'd landed here... snug against him. Questions must be asked. Crucial ones like: where was she? Who was he? And most important—why couldn't she remember getting into his bed?

The inquiry jumpstarted her brain.

Ivy glanced at him from the corner of her eye. Her breath stalled in her throat. Lordy-lord- lord, he was gorgeous. So handsome with his dark hair, aristocratic features, and the day old stubble shadowing his jaw.

He twitched against her.

"Don't move. Stay still," she muttered under her breath, talking to herself, but mostly to him.

She didn't want him to wake up. The second he opened his eyes, she'd land in serious trouble. A bit dramatic on the reaction front? No. Absolutely not.

The size of him helped her gauge the threat level. Too big. Crazy muscular. A billion times stronger than her.

Red...she was at *threat level RED*.

Time to leave.

She needed to facilitate an escape. Right now. A quick sideways slide to the edge of the bed. A faster dash toward the door and... Ivy glanced over her shoulder.

Crap. It was too dark. With nothing but the weak glow of a fish tank across the room, she couldn't see the exit. Her gaze darted to the bedside table. The faint outline of a lamp taunted her. Damn it. The stupid thing was too far away. She couldn't flip the light on without reaching over him.

Oh man. She was so screwed.

The instant she moved, he'd wake up and try to stop her. Instinct told her so. Intuition laid out the rest of the plan. Or rather, her downfall in stunning clarity. Which was odd since she couldn't recall anything else. A fractured image rose in her mind's eye. Her gaze trailed over the strong lines of his face and landed on his throat.

Her focus sharpened another notch.

She remembered that spot, the place where his pulse throbbed beneath scratchy stubble. She'd tasted it last night. Had set her mouth to the side of his neck, felt his carotid artery beat against the tip of her tongue and given in to the sizzle of physical attraction. Shock thrummed through her. She sucked in a quick breath. Holy hell. The courtyard.

Something about a fountain, entwined snakes and...

She blinked as recollection failed her.

Ivy chased the memory anyway, struggling to put the piece together. Imagery flashed inside her head.

The facts gathered. Like black and white dominoes, each stood on end, lining up in military formation. The first one fell—the set up in Maryland, running from the FBI, Scotland, the cemetery, Tydrin and—

Her brain kicked over.

She jerked against him.

A dragon. She remembered him turning into a *dragon*.

Tydrin shifted in his sleep. His hold on her tightened before he settled again. Self- preservation flipped to the ON position. Panic powered up. Afraid to breath, Ivy remained frozen against him. The wrong reaction. Completely idiotic in terms of plan implementation. She needed to go right now. Run. Hide. Get away for good.

Common sense dictated the path, and yet, she didn't move. She stayed still instead, fighting the undeniable urge to lay her head back down. Soak up more of his heat. Revel in the strength of his body. Feel safe with him instead of threatened.

Which left two options.

Put out an all points gorgeous guy alert and get busy exploring. Or find the nearest doctor and have her head examined.

The second idea seemed like a better option. An MRI might be required. A regular dose of anti-psychotics worked wonders for some people. Maybe it would for her. Knowing she tumbled toward crazy, however, didn't cure the infatuation. She couldn't stop staring at him. There was something about him. Something comforting. Something familiar and safe.

Forget all the weirdness.

Set aside the dragon stuff for a second.

A stark realization ramped up, requiring her attention. Maybe it was the lethal vibe he threw off like pheromones. Perhaps it was the peaceful way he slept. Or the feel of his hard body against hers. Ivy didn't know, but...wow. Waking up next to him qualified as an interesting first for her.

Guys who looked like Tydrin didn't crawl into her bed. Or tuck her into theirs.

Ivy snorted. Uh-huh. Right. As if hotties like him ever went for girls like her. International cover models, sure. Long, leggy blondes with killer bods and perfect skin? Absolutely. Curvy redheads with more freckles than good sense? Not really. She'd wager the occurrence appeared closer to *never* on the sliding date-me scale than *remotely possible*.

Her geekiness scared men away.

Too much brain power for them, maybe. Less social skills than a yak in heat, perhaps. Not that it mattered. The reasons could wait while she figured out her attraction to Tydrin. But as she watched him sleep —chest rising and falling under her hand—comprehension abandoned her. Confusion bombarded her instead. It was odd. So strange that she wasn't afraid of him. Ivy worried the inside of her bottom lip with her teeth. All right, so the man-dragon angle concerned her. Dragons, after all, weren't supposed to exist. Not outside the realm of on-line gaming communities anyway. Still, she couldn't deny what she'd witnessed.

Or that he'd saved her life.

Toss in the fact her chest didn't hurt anymore and...

Ivy frowned. Crazy that she hadn't realized it until now, but...she could breathe. Really *breathe* for the first time in years. She couldn't remember a time when she'd been pain-free or woken without needing her medicine. Getting enough air had always been a big struggle. Until now. One night with Tydrin, and everything had changed.

Testing the theory, Ivy drew a deep breath.

Her lungs filled.

Her chest expanded.

She exhaled smooth and inhaled again, assessing her lung capacity. Oxygen flowed in. Carbon dioxide flowed out. Not an ounce of discomfort. No need to reach for her inhaler. All systems go, two thumbs way, *way* up.

She dropped her gaze to the quilt. Navy blue threads dotted the material, drawing patterns across the white cotton. Lifting her hand from Tydrin's chest, she traced the swirl of curving lines. Her fingernail rasped over stitches sewn by a steady hand.

Straight. Narrow. Perfect in every way.

Unlike the mess she'd made of her life.

"Ivy." Fingers touched the furrow between her brows.

She flinched.

Tydrin paused, a fingertip poised above her skin, then continued, caressing her as though he had the right. A feathered touch over the arch of her eyebrow. The soft brush of his thumb against her cheek. His hand cupping her jaw as he tipped her chin up. Dark purple eyes captured hers.

She shivered.

His mouth curved. "Wool gathering, are ye?"

"Seems like the thing to do." Unable to look away, Ivy weighed her next words with care. She didn't want to piss him off. Or be disrespectful. Something told her that wouldn't go over well. Not with Tydrin. He might be patient. Might even be gentle with her, but only an idiot would ignore his tendency toward aggression. It didn't take a genius to know he was lethal.

And far too close— awake and aware—for her to make a clean escape. Still, she refused to shy away. Avoiding the topic wouldn't help clarify things. Honesty, however, just might. "Considering you're a dragon."

"Only half, lovely." Eyes crinkling at the corners, he tapped her bottom lip. "The other fifty percent is all human."

Incredulity struck.

Ivy opened her mouth.

No sound came out.

Clearing her throat, she tried again. "How can that be? I mean...what...where...I just...dragons are not supposed to exist."

"Anonymity, Ivy. 'Tis the way we like it."

"We?"

"Dragonkind."

"I don't understand."

"'Tisn't complicated," he said, picking up a lock of her hair. He lingered a moment, twirling the strands around his finger before tucking it behind her ear. "Dragonkind is simply another species on a planet full of them. Like humans and birds and panda bears. No different."

"Not the same either."

"True."

"Why the anonymity?"

He shrugged, jostling her as he stuffed a pillow under his head. "Staying hidden is important. Better for us. Safer for humans in the long run too."

"Kind of like—if we knew, you'd have to kill us?"

He snorted in amusement. "Now you're getting it."

She rolled her eyes. Charming jerk. It was difficult not to like him. Even harder to be afraid when he smiled at her like that. "Do you wield magic?"

"Aye. Every day."

"Did you use it on me last night?" she asked, curiosity driving her into the conversation instead of away.

And yet, the need to move away from him nudged her.

Lying next to him wasn't a good idea. She needed distance. Enough to force her brain to work. Enough to think rationally, with her head, not her libido.

Pushing at the covers, Ivy shifted, each movement measured as she pulled back. She settled on her knees a few feet away. Her bottom touched her heels. The mattress sighed underneath her. Tydrin didn't say a word. He watched instead, letting her go without argument.

A terrific concession. A smart decision. One designed to settle her nerves.

Even so, his lazy façade didn't fool her. He was in control. Bigger. Stronger. Faster. Able to draw her back to his side whenever he wanted.

Chewing on her bottom lip, she studied him. "Is magic what I felt when you landed in the courtyard."

He raised a brow. "I touched you with human hands?"

She nodded.

Elbows bent, fingers laced behind his head, he studied her from beneath his dark lashes. The silence stretched, upping her tension as he sat up. Ivy slid backward another foot, heading for the edge of the mattress. He murmured a reassurance and stopped advancing in favor of sitting cross-legged in front of her.

"Sorry," she whispered, feeling bad for retreating. "It's not that I think you'll hurt me or anything, but..." She swallowed, pausing to gather her thoughts. "I just don't know you very well."

"'Tis all right, lass." His mouth curved. "You've not hurt my feelings."

"Well, that's a relief," she said, sarcasm out in full force.

He laughed.

Her stomach flip-flopped at the sound. So deep. So attractive. So enthralling that—Ivy frowned. Crap. Wrong thought. Bad libido, but...man. Tydrin was beautiful. His appeal flipped her switch, prompting all kinds of naughty thoughts.

The kind a girl couldn't ignore.

Ivy grimaced. Hot and bothered. Ready and willing. Talk about a terrible idea. Her inner sex kitten didn't care. The little minx refused to give her a break, tossing out inappropriate suggestions that ended with her legs wrapped around Tydrin's waist...every single time.

"Traitor," Ivy muttered, struggling to subdue her out-of-control inner vixen. Laughter in his eyes, Tydrin titled his head. "What was that, lass?"

"Nothing." Heat rose in her cheeks. Tamping down her embarrassment, Ivy dragged her mind out of the gutter and tipped her chin. "So about the magic?"

"Right," he murmured, frowning a little. "'Tis hard tae explain, but what you felt is not ordinary, Ivy. 'Tis unusual. A rare blending of energies for my kind. The strength of it allowed me to share my life-force with you. Tae target the weakness in your lungs and heal it."

*Life force? Targeting of illnesses?*

Her brows popped up. Seriously?

Struggling to piece it together, she sorted through the information he offered. All right. Maybe. She could buy it on some level. The energy exchange seemed plausible. She'd felt it—the surge, the awareness, the raw heat as he'd caressed her in the courtyard. "Am I cured then? No more asthma?"

"No more asthma," he said, mimicking her quiet tone.

Gratefulness swamped her.

Tears filled her eyes.

"I don't know what to say. I just...I mean, other than thank you." Pressing her palm over her breastbone—the place it always hurt the most—Ivy lost the battle. Free and clear. One hundred percent healed. No more struggling. Emotion escaped along with her tears. Droplets rolled over her bottom lashes and down her cheeks as she held his gaze. "Thank you, Tydrin. I can't tell you...you have no idea how good it feels to breathe without pain. It was getting worse and I was so worried."

Her voice cracked on the last word.

"Sweet, sweet lass." Raising his hands, he cupped her face and urged her closer.

She shuffled across the quilt, going without complaint, closing the distance, surrendering control. He hummed in appreciation. She whispered his name as he wiped her tears away. His gaze raked her face. Desire curled in the pit of her stomach. Her lips parted without prompting.

Accepting the invitation, Tydrin leaned in and kissed her softly.

Ivy moaned. Oh blessed day. Sweet soul-stealing calamity. He tasted good, like moonbeams, milk chocolate and deep, dark passion.

Holding her in his hands, he retreated enough to

look at her. "Your pleasure is mine, Ivy. We may have just met, but you mean the world tae me. I'll do whatever it takes tae keep you healthy and safe."

Another round of tears threatened. How incredible. What an amazing thing to say. He was a revelation. A real life knight-in-shining-armor, and far too good to be true.

Caution raised all kinds of red flags, telling her to be careful.

He wasn't a normal guy.

She wasn't part of his world.

But sitting with him, staring at him, talking to him, she couldn't make herself care. The warning signs didn't matter. Neither did the fact she might be stepping into a world of hurt, delivering a self-inflected wound.

She wanted him.

Just for tonight. Just for here and now. Or however long life allowed her to have him.

She needed to believe someone wanted her. Valued her. Respected her. Desired her so much he would drop everything to be with her. A foolish notion. She knew it. Accepted it. Twenty-first century women didn't welcome saviors. Here, though— right now, in this moment—Ivy left her preconceived notion behind. What the world expected, what others preached—who a woman was supposed to be, what she ought to do—could go hang itself.

She craved the connection. Needed his touch. Yearned for his taste. Longed to press her body to his —feel his hands on her skin—and forget her problems...if only for a little while.

"Tydrin?"

"Aye, lovely?"

"I remember now. You promised me something last night." His eyes began to shimmer. "Did I?"

"Yes," she said, feeling shy, but not enough to back down. She stood on the edge of a precipice. A ledge with two choices: retreat to safety or jump in without hesitation. God forgive her. She wanted to make the leap, fall fast, hit hard, lose herself in the longing. Holding his gaze, Ivy drew a deep breath. Now or never. Be brave or stay scared. It took her a split second to decide. "You said that if I let you, you'd make love to me. Is that still true?"

"More than ever."

"Time to keep your word."

Desire darkened the purple flecks in his eyes. His nostrils flared a second before he surged toward her. His grip firmed. His body flexed. Ivy gasped as Tydrin took control and flipped her over.

She landed on her back.

He came down on top of her.

Rigid with arousal, he pressed down, giving her his weight as he settled between the spread of her thighs. "Do you want me, Ivy?"

"Yes."

"Can you feel how much I want you?" he asked, his chest against hers.

Her nipples peeked. "You know I can."

"Then be sure, lovely." Shackling her wrists, Tydrin pulled her arms above her head. He held her there, legs spread, hands pressed to the bed, mouth a hair's breadth from hers. Expression set, he swiveled his hips. Pleasure spiked. Tipping her head back, she arched, shuddering against him. "Once we start—the instant I get a proper taste of you—I might not be able tae stop."

"I'm sure. Tydrin, I'm sure." Half-drunk on his

scent, in need of his taste, she tugged on her hands, begging without words to be released. She needed to touch him—to feel, explore, give as good as he gave.

He shook his head, denying her silent request, and rolled his hips again.

Bliss rumbled through her, making her moan beneath him. "No stopping. I want all you have to give."

"Thank Christ."

The low growl sounded in her ear. His eyes sparked, shimmering purple in the dark, and Ivy let herself go. She was Tydrin's for the moment. His for the taking. His to please in whatever ways he wanted. His without apology as he dipped his head and invaded her mouth.

# 7

**T**HE INSTANT he got his first taste of her, Tydrin fell from grace and straight into heaven. He growled as Ivy shifted underneath him and...oh baby. Blessed be the day. He must've been born under a lucky star. Or singled out by the most forgiving of angels. Whatever. The reason for his good fortune didn't matter. Label it time off for good behavior. Call it emotional parole. Place addiction at the top of the list.

Only one thing mattered—Ivy and what she made him feel.

Without effort, she tipped the scales, upending him, blowing past rational to shove him straight into enthrallment. Now he reeled, head spinning, body humming, a prisoner of desire as he deepened the kiss and took what she offered.

Everything she gave.

All he wanted too.

Which made him a first class cad.

He shouldn't be kissing her like this. Shouldn't be nestled between her thighs and pressed to her core. Shouldn't be chest to breast with her, hands threaded in her hair while he tangled his tongue with hers either. Not before they talked and he came clean. Told her who he was and what he'd done, but...

Goddess help him.

She tasted so good. Felt amazing—all lush curves, soft skin and glorious passion. Now, he couldn't pull away. Couldn't force his muscles to unlock long enough to let her go. Not that he wasn't trying, but—

His dragon half refused to listen.

Charmed by her, the unscrupulous beast dug in, locking him in place, controlling the play, demanding he please the female in his arms. Another reason to call himself a bastard. Touching her—loving her— wasn't right. She needed to know the truth before he went any further.

The human side of him nodded. His dragon continued to disagree, pointing to one indisputable fact. Ivy wanted him. Needed him. Might even yearn for him as much as he did her, so...screw it. His conscience could go hang itself. Right. Wrong. Neither passed muster anymore. All that mattered was her and what she asked of him.

Pleasure, hot and devastating, poured through him.

His heart slammed against the inside of his chest. The blood rush spiked, and...hmm, so good. She was incredible. So glorious in her passion. So beautiful in her need. So hot she took his breath away, turning him inside out with each sexy sound she made.

The instant one breathy moan ceased, he wanted her to make another. And then more after that. The compulsion to hear her scream his name as she came cranked him tight. The lockdown pushed past self-imposed boundaries, threatening his control. Now he didn't know what to do—give her what she demanded, a fast, hard loving. Or slow down long enough to explore every gorgeous inch of her.

Slow suited him better.

He liked to take his time. Loved hearing a female beg while he watched her squirm. Adored the slide of satiny skin beneath his hands. Enjoyed the taste and scent of a female in the full bloom of arousal. Always made a fast getaway after he finished pleasing her too. Hunt with purpose. Chase with charm. Conquer without mercy. A tried and true method for Dragonkind males when dealing with women.

His MO down to the letter. Until now.

Until Ivy.

She presented him with a different set of possibilities. More opportunities too. Precious. Special. A gift given at the eleventh hour. She was the kind of female a smart male never took for granted. Precisely how it should be. Why? Unlike the females he'd pleasured in the past, Ivy belonged to him. Was *his* in every sense of the word. His to comfort and protect. His to love and please. His to house and hold. Which meant...

No way would he rush the encounter.

He wanted to feel everything. Remember each moment. Experience her—and their first time together—to the fullest.

Every second of the next few hours counted. His undying need. Her complete satisfaction. The ecstasy he would give her while receiving his own. All of it mattered, so...aye. Without a doubt. Time to pull his head out of his arse and get with the program. Before he pushed too hard. Before he went too fast and lost all control.

Grabbing the frayed ends of his restraint, Tydrin retreated, lessening the pressure.

Ivy whimpered in protest.

The sound slid through his veins, slicing at his willpower. The tethers holding him in check unraveled. Lust escalated. Conviction took a nose dive and... shite. He was in serious trouble. Exposed in a world where rapture ruled and males bowed down, surrendering to unparalleled bliss. Digging in, he bore down, struggling to lift his mouth from hers long enough to reestablish control.

An excellent plan, but for one teeny-tiny problem.

Ivy had other ideas.

Refusing to let him go, she fisted her hands in his hair. An instant later, she upped the ante, locking her legs around his waist. Intense heat scorched him. His brain derailed, sliding off mental tracks. Tydrin deepened the kiss. With a moan, she tightened her grip. Short nails scraped over his scalp. Delight blew sky high. Prickles exploded down his spine. Showing no mercy, Ivy undulated beneath him.

Shuddering in her arms, Tydrin wrenched his mouth from hers. "Ivy."

Ignoring him, she arched and set her lips back on his.

Tydrin cursed and kissed her again. Fucking hell. Had he said trouble earlier? Well, triple the effect. She was diabolical, moving way too fast, pulling him far too deep, murdering his ability to resist her with a kiss. But my oh my, what a mouth. Hot and full, so tasty he—

She sucked on his tongue.

"Bloody hell." Muffled by her mouth, the explicative came out weak. His reaction, however, was anything but. Locking his muscles, he cupped her face and, holding her in check, lifted his head.

His lips left hers.

She murmured his name.

He bared his teeth. "Ivy!"

"Don't."

"Donnae what?"

"Stop," she said, tone full of fear.

Tydrin frowned as her disquiet registered, hitting him like a closed fist. He inhaled a quick breath. What the hell? He wanted her compliant—to slow down long enough for him to explain the ground rules—not afraid, but... shite. He saw the dread on her face, in her eyes and the way she stiffened beneath him too.

"You said you wouldn't," she whispered, now tense beneath him. "Tydrin, you promised."

"Sweet lass, I'm not. I've no wish tae stop. I couldn't now if I tried, but—"

"No buts." Her voice hitched, breaking his heart. "Do you have any idea how long it's been since I've been with a guy? Since I've had any pleasure at all?"

He blinked. "How long?"

"Seems like forever. Years." A furrow between her brows, hands resting on his shoulders, she stared up at him. "Asthma makes everything difficult. I have trouble catching my breath when I get...excited."

Her cheeks heated with the admission. Color spread over her cheekbones in crimson wave.

Held hostage by the sight, Tydrin swallowed a groan as the freckles sprinkled over the bridge of her nose grew rosy. He blew out a shaky breath. Sugar. The alluring flecks on her skin reminded him of sprinkled sugar, and damned if he didn't plan on tasting each and every one.

Breaking eye contact, she looked away. "The second I reach for my inhaler, the guy always freaks out, and well, the mood gets ruined."

"The mood isnae ruined. Far from it." Drawing gentle circles on her skin, he brushed a tangle of dark red tendrils away from her temple. "I want you, Ivy. I intend tae have you...more than once today, but—"

"I hate that word."

He ignored the interruption. "I need tae slow down, luv. A male only has so much control, and I want tae enjoy every second of you. I crave your skin against mine. I long tae learn your shape and worship every curve. I need tae taste your passion before I lose myself in the loving. 'Tisn't a question of want, lovely. I *need* it that way. Naught else will satisfy me. But if we keep on like this—the pace hot and fast—I'll not last long enough tae please you."

"Oh. Well..." Surprise winged across her face. After a moment, the shock in her eyes faded.

A mischievous glint replaced it. "All right, then. Lead on. You have my permission."

"Your *permission*?" He snorted. Plucky lass. Tempestuous wee tease. She didn't know how much her challenge turned him on. Or what happened when a female provoked his dragon half with such deliberate intent. "Insubordination, lass. I'll make you pay for it."

"Maybe. Or maybe, I'll make you beg."

"Unlikely," he said, sounding confident even though he didn't believe it. Ivy held the power to bring him to his knees. It wouldn't take much. The husky sound of her voice. The lush curves of her body. The heated gleam in her eyes. With little effort, she could undo him. Tydrin knew it. Should be wary of it. Acknowledging it, however, ranked low on his list of priorities. He was here. She was ready to take him all the way. Too hell with the consequences. "We'll see how long you last, lovely. You'll beg—eventually."

"Dream on, handsome."

"No need. I plan tae make you scream in pleasure."

"Hallelujah. About time somebody did."

He grinned.

She smiled back, and he was right back to being lost. Totally fucking *lost*. He couldn't get enough of her. He'd barely touched her. Hadn't managed to get her naked yet, and he was already gone. On edge. In too deep. So amped up he didn't know what to do first —thank the Goddess for planting her in his path or attack her clothes and strip her bare.

Tydrin opted to do both and grabbed the bottom of her T-shirt. Ivy raised her arms. He pulled the stretchy cotton up her torso and over her head.

A racy white bra came into view.

Tydrin groaned. Oh man, look at her. *Just look at her.* So unabashed as he uncovered her.

Too beautiful for words. Beyond tempting for a male gone hungry for too long.

One hundred percent his for the taking.

The realization spoke to his heart, tempting him to lay out the truth, leave himself vulnerable, hand her all the power. The silent message sank in, tempting him. An answering need surfaced as Ivy raised her hand. Fingertips stroking over his jaw, she tilted her hips, inviting his possession.

Holding her gaze, he pressed her back down, the urge to trust her with his secrets riding him hard. It would feel so good to give himself over. Surrender the past. Release the pain. Give Ivy the power to create an alternative reality. A new path for his future. One in which forgiveness granted him permission to be happy.

With her.

He knew she could do it. Banish the past. Forgive his mistakes. Slay all his demons. In some ways, she already had, freeing him from the self-imposed prison he locked himself inside every day.

The emotional shift startled him. He didn't deserve absolution—or merit release—and yet, Ivy made him believe. Despite his imperfections, she lay in his bed, the key to his heart in her hand, the promise of his future in her eyes. And as his fingertips traced the lace covering breast, Tydrin held her gaze and let go, allowing her access to parts of him he hadn't known existed.

Not until now. Never before her.

## 8

THE DESIRE in Tydrin's eyes threatened to unhinge her. Her heart throbbed, kicking hard as he trailed his fingers over the lace edging her bra. She shuddered beneath him. He continued to tease, his gentle touch designed for one purpose—to amp her up and drive her crazy.

A great plan.

At least, for him.

For her, it was fast becoming more complicated. With each barely there caress, she lost a little more of her mind. His soft groans of appreciation weren't helping. The praise he whispered, calling her beautiful, telling her how much he wanted her and—

Just like that, it was over.

She was done. Beyond help. Torn open, exposed in an emotional landscape with a target on her back. Point and shoot, 'cause...wow. She'd been hit, and had become wholly his. Ensnared by the look in his eyes. Enthralled by the timbre of his voice as she struggled to do as he asked and be patient.

*Patience.* Such a difficult thing to achieve.

She'd always been more of a doer. A giver, not a

taker. And guess what? Her *charge into the fray, get it done* attitude always served her well.

Until today.

Tydrin wasn't cooperating. He expected her to lay still and allow him to love her. The switch up—the denial of her type A personality—shoved her into uncharted territory, leaving her without a reference. Now she drifted, anchored only by him as he took his time, refusing to let her rush him.

Weird. Most guys couldn't wait to get inside a girl and the body-bumping bliss. But as Tydrin explored, feeding her more pleasure than she'd ever known, comprehension arrived. It knocked on her mental door and, as she opened it, Ivy finally understood.

She'd been asking all the wrong questions. She needed to reframe things, move toward important questions like: was sex supposed to be this good? Was it as fantastic for other people as it was for her right now? And lastly—why the hell hadn't she demanded pleasure like this from all those other guys?

Tydrin flicked her with his tongue, wetting her through the lace. Sensation crested in a wave of delight.

Ivy moaned. The hard edge of his teeth on her skin—the press of his hips between her thighs, the heat of his breath on her breast—felt so good. Beyond anything she'd ever experience and...all right. Time for a little honesty. *All those other guys*—the ones she'd mentioned earlier—qualified as a big fat lie. Ivy suppressed the urge to cringe. The sum total of her sexual experience consisted of two guys, one in high school, the other while working at INP Securities.

Neither had ended well.

Or given her half as much pleasure as Tydrin.

Awe sank deep. Tipping her head back, Ivy tried to

hold on, but...holy crap. The way he affected her was demented. Supernatural or something. Had to be. She couldn't find another explanation. Tydrin turned her into an inferno of need without even trying. Case in point? She wasn't even naked yet and she could feel the orgasm coming, bubbling up from hidden depths, scorching her with the rumble of approaching heat.

She squirmed, begging without words to be taken.

In no hurry, he fiddled at the front clasp of her bra and dipped his head. The heat of his mouth touched her. Her breath hitched. He flicked at her skin before stringing kisses over the top of her breast. She moaned his name. *Oh, yes, please. Come on.* She wanted him so badly. Needed what he promised. Teasing her, he tugged one strap off her shoulder. His mouth touched down again, following the slow slide of satin and lace and...

*Please, please, please...*

"Take it off." Breathing hard, she arched beneath him. "I want it off. All of it—*off*."

His mouth curved. "Naughty lass. Still think you're in charge, do ye?"

She scowled at him. "Tydrin."

"I thought we agreed you'd be patient."

"I thought we agreed you'd give me an orgasm."

He chuckled. "Oh, we'll get tae that, lovely."

"Before or after I go insane?"

"Impatient lass."

"I'm sorry," she whispered in genuine remorse.

She'd promised not to rush him, to lay back and let him lead, but desperation made a girl do crazy things—like push a man-dragon into making love to her. Bold to the next power. Probably not the wisest move, all things considered. Ivy didn't care. She couldn't wait much longer. He made her feel too much, yet not nearly enough. Everything and nothing at all.

"I need you, Tydrin. I don't think I can handle slow the first time."

"The first time," he repeated, tone low and soft.

Lifting his head, he focused on her face. He studied a second before his gaze dipped to the aroused points of her nipples. He watched her breathe, registering the quick rise and fall of her chest, reading her need, letting her see his own. Desire heightened the color riding the edge of his cheekbones. The shimmer in his eyes intensified, painting her in purple wash. Excitement skittered down her spine as Tydrin bared his teeth on a growl. "All right, lass. You win. Faster this time, slower the second."

"Thank you."

"My pleasure," he said, kissing her. "Everything about you is a pleasure."

Pride swamped her. Self-confidence followed fast on its heels. So nice. Beautiful without end. He wanted her. Really *wanted* her. He was a dream come true, a man willing to forgo his needs in favor of assuaging hers.

Raising her hand, she cupped his face. "You're the incredible one."

He shook his head and planted his hands on either side of her. The mattress dipped as he pushed up. The sheet fell away, baring his body. She sucked in a quick breath as her eyes roamed. Oh glory days. He was gorgeous, all hard muscle and golden skin. Long, strong and lean. A wide-shouldered, hard-bodied dream.

Unable to stop staring, she looked her fill. Tydrin let her, staying still as her gaze trailed lower and... umm. Would you look at that? Pure male perfection standing at attention. Hot and hard and ready, one hundred percent committed to her pleasure.

She licked her bottom lip. Her eyes rose to meet his. She reached out. "I want to taste you."

He caught her wrist, stopping her from touching him. "Not this time."

"But—"

"Later. You get that gorgeous mouth anywhere near me right now, and I willnae last."

Pushing out her bottom lip, she pouted.

He grinned and, shaking his head, threw his leg over her. Straddling her hips, towering over her, he ran his finger down the center of her chest. She arched beneath the teasing caress. He paused, hovering over her breasts before flicking at her bra. "Take it off for me."

Ivy didn't hesitate.

She reached for the front clasp. Hard plastic slid against her fingertips. She fumbled a second, struggling to undo a fastening she opened and closed every day. Frustration rose. Ivy shoved it back down. No need for any of that. Not right now. She refused to become flustered with Tydrin watching. She longed to please him. Show him how much she wanted him. Be the one to surrender. Give him all he asked and everything he needed.

Feeling for the seam, she tried again.

The clasp gave way with a click.

Determined to be bold, she drew the lace aside, uncovering herself, watching him watch her. Cold air washed over her skin. Furled into tight buds, her nipples tingled, begging for the heat of his mouth.

"Gorgeous." His lips parted on a ragged intake of breath. "You're beautiful, Ivy. Every last inch of you."

Politesse urged her to thank him again. Held captive by his reaction, Ivy swallowed her reply in favor of staying quiet. No sense chancing it. She refused to break the mood. Not with him staring at her with longing in his eyes. The sight of his need heightened her own. Lust narrowed its focus, funneling into desperation.

Ivy wiggled her hips, urging him on. She needed his touch, for him open the flood gates of desire and teach her about passion. Show her the real kind. The hot burn instinct insisted she'd never once experienced. Not before tonight. Never before him. Her illness made exercise and exertion difficult. Almost impossible. A huge disappointment, the defining factor in her sexual evolution. She'd suffered the limitation all her life.

But not anymore.

Tydrin had taken care of the problem, freeing her from asthmatic chains. Now she could feel to her heart's content. Let go of the fear. Delve deep into blistering need. Burn hot beneath his hands and give as good as Tydrin gave her.

He shifted, dismounting to kneel beside her. "Lift up."

Pressing her shoulders into the rumpled quilt, Ivy raised her bottom off the bed. The button of her jeans popped. His callused fingertips brushed her belly. Bliss whispered her name as Tydrin grasped her zipper. The quiet zing of metal on metal broke through the quiet. The muscular planes of his chest rose and fell as he tugged at her jeans. Denim slipped over her hips and down her thighs. He groaned and reached out to cup her mound. The tips of his fingers stroked lower, caressing her through the cotton.

"God, yes."

"Hmm, so hot, Ivy. So slick," he said, voice low and raspy. "You're soaked, so fucking wet."

Undulating against the heel of his hand, she bit down on a moan. "Told you I couldn't wait."

"So I see and..." Trailing off, he hooked his fingers in her panties. With a tug, he drew the frilly cotton down her legs. Goosebumps pebbled her skin as he threw her clothes over the side of the bed. "I'm no better. I cannae go slow any longer, lass. I want you too much."

"Perfect."

"Spread your legs."

Raising her knees, Ivy splayed her thighs open for him.

Gaze riveted to her, he smoothed his hands up her calves. Big hands cupped the backs of her legs, then skimmed higher. Need spiked. Her heart picked up the beat, rushing blood through her veins. Inner muscles pulsed, tightening her deep inside. The delightful throb thrust her hips up. With a groan, Tydrin pressed her knees up and out, spread her wider, preparing her for his touch.

His fingers brushed the curls between her thighs. She gasped as he sank between her folds, playing in her slickness, exploring her completely, pressing deeper with each caress.

Ivy bucked against his hand. Oh God. Heat lightening. Pure bliss. Huge, *huge* pleasure from each mind-blowing stroke.

Tydrin caressed her again. And then again. Over and over. No end in sight. Zero relief on the horizon as he learned her shape. He exposed her clit. She froze, breath stalled in her throat as he circled the sensitive nub with the pad of his thumb, then thrust one finger deep. Ivy threw her head back and her hips up. She needed more. More pressure. Deeper contact. All the bliss his fingers promised. Right now. Before she started begging out loud.

He pumped his hand. Thrust and withdraw. Advance and retreat. The diabolical rhythm drove her wild, but kept her on edge, never quite cresting. Now she teetered on the precipice— primed and desperate, a shimmer away from orgasm.

"Tydrin!"

"Ah, there it 'tis. I've almost got you begging." He growled the last word and shifted toward her. "Come on, Ivy—beg me."

"Please!" Her plea echoed in the quiet of the room. To hell with it. She didn't care anymore. She craved the ecstasy. Wanted him thick and deep inside her. Needed the advance and retreat more than her next breath. Her pride could go to hell along with her convictions. "Please, please...*please*!"

"Grab the edge of the mattress."

She reached above her head and took hold. The position thrust her breasts up. Withdrawing his hand, Tydrin settled between her thighs and took advantage. His head dipped. Soft as angel wings, his hair brushed across her breastbone. The heat of his mouth washed over her skin. Rapture whispered and sensation whiplashed, burning her from the inside out as he licked her nipple.

He suckled the tight bud, drawing pleasure through her pores.

Twisting beneath him, Ivy keened.

"Hang on tight, lovely," he whispered, tongue playing at her breast. "It's going tae be a wild, hard ride."

Panting, so needy she couldn't talk, Ivy tightened her grip. Tydrin set himself at her entrance and thrust inside. Her inner muscles stretched, struggling to accommodate him. He showed no mercy. With a growl, he conquered her, lighting up pleasure pathways, stealing her breath every time his pelvis met hers.

Delight whipped through her.

Need escalated and caught fire. She wrapped her legs around him.

He groaned her name.

She whispered back and, burying her hands in his hair, arched into his next thrust. Hard. Fast. Powerful personified. True to his word, he took her hard, sparking a desire-fueled inferno as he plunged deep, then retreated, rocking her in his arms.

"Oh God. Oh yes. Wow, wow, wow," she said, each word a benediction.

"Ivy. Bloody hell—Ivy!"

"More, more, more," she panted, holding on tight.

"Come for me." Body slick with sweat, he upped the pace. His hips slammed into hers, lifting her off the bed. "Please, Ivy-mine, come for me."

His plea unleashed her.

Ivy detonated, screaming as she came. He tightened around her. His breath rasped from his throat. Thrusting one last time, he pressed deep, held firm and—

He groaned her name.

She cried out as he pulsed inside her. God, yes. Sing it, sister. She'd done it. Given him so much pleasure he couldn't let her go. He held on tight instead, voice hoarse with wonder as he whispered her name —over and over, again and again.

Greedy in the aftermath, he kept her close, skin-to-skin and heart-to-heart, showing her the meaning of connection for the first time in her life. Emotion reached through the breach, and Ivy knew. She recognized the shift. Felt the undeniable pull, and no matter how unwise, couldn't deny him.

He wanted her near. She needed to be right where she was—wrapped in his arms.

A dangerous compulsion. A terrible threat to her peace of mind, an unwise risk to her heart. It didn't matter. Here...right now...she welcomed him without fear. Lost more of herself. Accepted that throwing up psychological barricades and fleeing behind mental walls into self-protection would never work. It was too late for retreat. Her defenses were down. Now she couldn't walk away.

Foolish, perhaps. A mistake in the making, no doubt.

Retreat would be smarter. A little vigilance, after all, went a long way. But even as the idea formed, Ivy acknowledged the futility.

Meeting Tydrin might have been a fluke, but making love with him wasn't a mistake. She belonged in his arms. He belonged in hers. And as he nestled in, snuggling closer, an abiding truth took hold. He felt right. Was the perfect fit, touching a place inside her where souls dovetailed and love conquered all. So onward and upward. Time to shove caution aside. Right. Wrong. Neither applied anymore. She refused to run away. She'd keep him close instead, enjoy every second of him—for as long as the powers-that-be allowed.

# 9

**F**LAT ON HIS back on his side of the bed, a rumpled sheet around his waist and a satisfied female asleep at his side, Tydrin sighed in contentment. Hmm, unbelievable. It felt so good to lie back in near darkness and relax for a while. For the first time in what seemed like forever.

To be expected.

Pretty accurate time wise.

His brain never turned off, not even during the day while he slept. Like a hamster on a wheel, his mind whirled at breakneck speed, sprinting from one thought to the next, never allowing him to unwind.

Sad in some ways. Well-earned in others.

He didn't deserve the relief. Hadn't earned his leisure. The ugliness of his past said as much. The guilt he carried like a loadstone proved it, eating at him, hollowing him out until emptiness threatened and nothing good remained.

But not right now.

The mental slowdown drew him into enjoyment.

Muscles lax and eyes closed, Tydrin drifted further into relaxation. The reprieve gave him hope. The reason behind it brought him peace. And the woman responsible for it all? An image of her—spine bowed in supplication as he made love to her—formed in his mind's eye. Gratitude gripped his heart.

Thank God for her.

Beautiful Ivy. Feisty wee lass with the indomitable spirit and lush body. Her presence drove his demons away, returned his faith, filled the massive hole in the center of his life, gifting him with the promise of a better future.

He turned his head on the pillow.

Cotton rustled against his ear as he glanced her way. Light from the fish tank across the room reached out to touch her face. Another round of contentment ghosted through him. Air left his chest in a rush. Bloody hell, not his imagination at all. There she was, his dream girl—Ivy of the messy red hair, pulse-raising pale skin and uber-keen mind.

His gaze left her face to roam her bare breasts.

Volcanic need surged, hardening him beneath the sheet. Again. Like always. Hard as a pike appeared to be his default setting whenever he looked at her. The thought made him smile. He shook his head and, rolling onto his side, propped himself up on one elbow to watch her sleep.

Exhausted by his constant need all afternoon, she lay half covered, the sheet at her waist, thick lashes curved in half-moons against her cheeks. Raising his hand, Tydrin traced the gorgeous curve of her hip. She frowned in her sleep. Satisfaction scorched him as he continued to explore.

His palm slid over the flat expanse of her belly and up her ribcage. Ivy murmured his name. He swallowed a groan. Goddess, she was incredible. Hot as hell when he touched her. Crazy responsive when he slipped between her thighs. So welcoming she made him throb just thinking about the last round of loving.

Awe joined the happiness swimming in his veins.

Undone.

He was completely *undone* by her. In thrall, under her spell, unraveling into a messy emotional tangle, but...whatever. His reaction to her didn't require a label. Well, except for one. Energy-fuse, the magical bond between a Dragonkind male and his mate. Rooted in magic. Unbreakable once created. A precious energy pairing forged by the Meridian.

The wonder of it tightened his chest.

Tydrin drew a steadying breath. How amazing. One in a million odds. A long shot most warriors never got to take. Good thing he wasn't most. For some reason, the universe smiled down on him. Now he knew. No sense fighting it. He'd been caught the moment he'd laid eyes on Ivy in the cemetery. Now he'd fallen hard, his heart already given, in the hands of the only female made and meant for him.

A miracle, pure and perfect. More than he deserved given the sin he couldn't undo.

Turning his hand, he cupped her breast.

Ivy stirred beneath his palm. Her eyelashes flicked. The thick fringe lifted, and he got nailed by sleepy blue eyes.

She hummed, awakening beneath his touch. "Hi."

"Hey."

Her lips tipped up at the corners. "I think I might be dead."

He huffed in amusement. "Need me tae revive you?"

"Good God, no." With a grimace, she stretched,

bending her knees beneath the sheet. Fine cotton tented, rustling in protest. Ivy groaned. "I've got enough sore muscles as it is."

"How about a shower, then?"

"Hmm, hot water." She sighed, unabashed pleasure in the sound. "Yes, please."

He chuckled and, leaning in, planted his hand beside her shoulder, caging her in his arms. His mouth hovered over her breast. Ivy froze beneath him, muscles taut as she waited for him to make his move. Enjoying the taunt and her anticipation, he flicked the tip of her nipple with his tongue. Her breath hitched. He growled in satisfaction and, drawing away, rolled over her to reach the side of the bed.

His arse landed on the mattress edge a second before his feet hit the floor. "Up you get, lass."

"God," she said, a grumble in her voice. "You are such a tease."

"You love it."

"True." She sighed again. "Sad, but true."

Grinning at her over his shoulder, he shackled her wrist and pulled her upright. She settled beside him. He didn't let her rest long. Full of energy, so light of heart he could hardly stand himself, Tydrin lifted her onto her feet. She swayed against him. He pulled her close, waited until she caught her balance, then took her hand and towed her around the end of the bed.

Sidestepping the antique table beside his favorite armchair, he bypassed the fish tank and headed for the door across the room. "A quick shower, lovely. Wash and go. We need tae hurry."

Turning her palm, she laced her fingers with his. "Why?"

"The others are already gathering for the evening meal."

Her brows furrowed. "Others?"

"My family, the other males in my pack. 'Tis time you met them."

"Oh," she whispered, sounding unsure. She didn't stop moving, though. Her hand in his, she followed him into the bathroom. "Are they like you?"

Unleashing his magic, Tydrin sent out a mental command. The halogens powered up above his head. Light spilled, making Ivy squint, illuminating marble-clad walls and an enormous freestanding shower in the center of the room. Ivy's gaze strayed to the custom-made vanity sitting to one side. Built by a master carpenter eons ago, the antique was a tribute to his kind, dragons in flight carved into walnut panels, fangs bared, wings spread wide, the moon rising behind each one.

"Like me?"

She nodded.

"Dragonkind."

"Aye."

Avoiding his gaze, Ivy stared at the double sinks. Her throat worked as she swallowed. Hooked into her life-force, Tydrin registered the sudden shift in her energy. Too much tension. A flicker of fear. Unease tightened his chest. What the hell? A moment ago, she'd been relaxed and playful. Now she looked worried, a second away from true panic. Frowning, Tydrin set his finger beneath her chin. She resisted his touch, refusing the silent request.

He applied gentle pressure, turning her toward him. "Look at me, Ivy."

She hesitated.

He insisted, firming his grip on her chin.

Worried blue eyes met his.

Disquiet spiraled into concern. "What's wrong?"

She blew out a shaky breath. "Will they be upset that I'm here?"

Her question cracked him wide open. Compassion bled through the fissure, urging him to reassure and shield her. "Nay, lovely. Donnae worry so. My brothers-in-arms will love you."

Straight white teeth peaked out to worry her bottom lip. "You can't know that."

"Sure I can."

"How?"

"They'll love you because I already do."

She blinked as surprise winged across her face.

Tydrin smoothed his expression, smothering a grimace. Well, shite. So much for keeping his secret under wraps. Talk about bad timing. He hadn't meant to go all in, be so hardcore, all or nothing with her. Admitting his feelings this soon constituted a bad idea. The worst under present circumstances. The last thing he wanted to do was frighten her. Or rush her into a relationship she wasn't ready to accept.

At least, not yet.

Ivy needed time to adjust to him and what he wanted from her. His plan, up until three seconds ago, had gone something like: have her spend time in his world, help her become accustom to Dragonkind ways, pray she fell as hard and fast as he had for her. But as she drew in a soft breath, and he saw wonder bloom in her eyes, Tydrin wondered if telling her the truth hadn't been a mistake. Not that it mattered anymore. He'd already let the cat out of the bag. Now he refused to take back the declaration. Or retreat into emotional safety.

Time wouldn't change the facts.

He loved her. Aye, it might be a young love—one

not yet fully realized—but his dragon half made it clear. Today, tomorrow, a year from now, the time-frame wouldn't affect the outcome. His heart was set, and no matter what happened, he would always choose Ivy.

## 10

B ACK IN JEANS AND A T-SHIRT, Ivy wanted to plant her feet as Tydrin towed her toward the bedroom door. She resisted the impulse at the last second, managing to hang onto her manners —and avoid the corner of a wide-backed arm chair— but boy, it was hard.

Almost too close to call as panic pushed her buttons.

The urge to turn and run thrummed through her.

Excellent idea. Running. Hiding. Finding a place to lay low for a while ranked high on her to-do list. She wouldn't disappear for long. A week of downtime would do. A month would be preferable, but well... crap. Just crap. Her pesky sense of fair play rejected the plan, refusing to press her heels to the floor and put on the brakes.

Too bad, really.

A little resistance would go a long way right now.

The tension cranking her tight worsened. An ache bloomed behind her eyes, then circled round to hammer the base of her skull. Ivy grimaced. Wonderful. Headache territory. Not a great sign. The pain signaled trouble, pointing to an inescapable fact. She was in deep doo-doo, the kind that specialized in first meetings and high expectations.

Tydrin kept walking.

Ivy's brain continued churning. Why? Oh, nothing special—just a catastrophe in the making.

Tydrin wanted her to meet his family. *Her*—a girl with no social graces and zero idea how to interact with normal people, never mind a bunch of man-dragons. But even as she acknowledged the impending doom, she stayed silent, keeping her hand in Tydrin's, allowing him to open the door without protest.

Well-oiled hinges sighed.

Bright light spilled over the threshold, cutting a swathe across pale walls and hardwood floor. With a gentle tug, Tydrin drew her out of the bedroom. Mosaic tiles chilled the bottoms of her bare feet, heralding a new space and a switch in décor.

Nerves twisted her stomach into knots.

Courage forced her to move forward.

Okay. So the situation wasn't ideal, but it was too late to change it. She'd reached the point of no return. Now or never. She could do it—cling to politesse, meet the pack, and pray she didn't say anything stupid. Or act like a social invalid and embarrass Tydrin in the process.

Leveling her chin, she glanced around. Her jaw dropped. Holy Christmas and a thousand sparkling lights, talk about unexpected. Spectacular too. Head tipped back, she stared at the stained-glass dome rising overhead before returning her attention to the room. The expansive space screamed expensive. Centuries old too, with dark wood paneling and scarred, ancient-looking doors marching around the circular room.

Her gaze drifted right, toward the massive stone fireplace.

Built on ancient lines, the hearth followed the curve, spanning the entire wall. Flames ate at logs as big as tree trunks, licking between the charred stack, throwing the scent of peat moss into the air. Ivy breath it in. The woodsy aroma triggered a memory, reminding her of nights she'd sat at her father knee, listening while he read her a bedtime story in front of the fire.

Her mouth curved as the memory took hold. She hadn't thought about that in years. Forever, really. And yet as she took in Tydrin's home, the pleasant reminder calmed her, helping her settle back into her own skin.

All of this could be hers.

Tydrin had said as much. Asked her to stay in the semi-dark, voice coaxing while he made love to her, how he felt about her on full display.

Ivy swallowed the lump in her throat. God, she was such a jerk. She hadn't answered him. Hadn't know what to say or how to react to his invitation. Being with him—no matter how right it felt—was still so new. Shiny and bright. No wear and tear on their budding love affair at all. Which meant...

She needed to think it through. And take more time to decide.

On what, she wasn't exactly sure.

Staying with Tydrin seemed like a done deal. Was a no- brainer in some ways and a crazy plan in others. Which pointed to an indisputable—and somewhat scary—fact: she was falling hard and fast for a man-dragon. The realization circled. Ivy huffed. Foolish. Brainless. She was acting like an idiot, allowing herself to be drawn too deep, too fast, but—

Tydrin made it easy.

He refused to hide anything from her—answering her questions, opening up, sharing about himself—explaining the ins and outs of Dragonkind—without hesitation, making her feel special and needed, and yes, even loved.

Now she didn't want to deny him anything.

Even if the decision changed the course of her life.

For better. For worse.

Surprise, surprise, either scenario would be all right with her—just as long as she got to stay with him. And as Ivy looked around, taking in the luxury, she imagined herself living in the lair. One of the deep-seated armchairs in front of the fireplace would be her spot. The perfect place to curl up with her computer and wreak havoc on the internet.

She pursed her lips. Her gaze swung left, narrowing on the long couches lounging above a collection of Persian rugs. Hmm, one of those would work too. Odd, wasn't it? She could already see herself sitting there. Was making herself right at home, and why not? Despite the enormity of the space, the room was cozy. Ritzy sure, but comfortable too. Totally normal —more fancy hotel than supernatural bat cave—with old world charm and a distinctly human vibe.

Tydrin skirted an antique desk sitting to one side.

The abrupt shift knocked Ivy out of her thoughts and back into the present.

She drew a fortifying breath. Lord save and keep her. It was happening. Any moment now, it would happen. His brothers-in-arms would arrive and, despite her idiotic fantasy of claiming the perfect spot in the room, she would be screwed.

Instinct screeched at her, yelling *do something!*

Ivy scrambled to obey. She needed a plan, just in

case things went south. Stalling still seemed like a safest bet. Saner with an extra helping of advisable too, but well...damn it all. She didn't want to disappoint Tydrin. Particularly after he'd been so good to her—keeping her safe, letting her stay, loving her so well she still tingled in interesting places. But honestly —his family? Really? Ivy shivered and tightened her grip on his hand as personal history highlighted her nasty habit of bungling social situations.

"Umm, Tydrin?"

"Simmer down, lovely." He stopped walking and turned to face her. Untangling his hand from hers, he cupped her shoulders and started massaging. Tense muscles sighed in relief. Ivy swallowed a moan. God, she loved it when he touched her. It didn't matter how —or even why— but every time he got close she reacted the same way. With pleasure and all out acceptance, as though nothing better existed in the world. "It's going tae be fine."

"Define fine, because you know..." His fingers pressed down, hitting some magical spot, releasing more tension. After a second—or twenty—of complete bliss, she rebooted her brain, forcing it back on line. "Look, I know I'm being a wuss about this, but—"

"You are not."

"It doesn't feel all that *fine* to me," she said, finding his indignant tone endearing even as she ignored the interruption.

"You're nervous. Nothing wrong with that, Ivy, but donnae let it get the better of you. My brothers-in-arms arnae going tae—"

A door slammed across the room.

The bang echoed before dissipating beneath the dome.

"Ah, good. Perfect timing." The low, gravel-filled

voice killed the quiet, raising the fine hairs on the nape of her neck. Ivy went rigid beneath Tydrin's hands. Holy crap. Not good. She wasn't ready yet, and whoever stood at her back sounded scary. Like a maniac psycho killer, not *fine* at all by her standards. "Bring her over here, Tydrin. I need a closer look."

"Shite, Wallaig." Tydrin scowled at someone over the top of her head. "Have you no manners?"

"None I can find at the moment."

Tydrin sighed, the sound full of resignation. "You're a complete wanker."

The guy snorted. "Stop stalling, laddie. Get over here. Let's have a look at her."

Frozen in place, Ivy didn't turn around. She stared at Tydrin instead, refusing to acknowledge the man across the room. Wallaig, the grouchy sounding guy, could wait. She wanted her, ah...she frowned. What in God's name should she call Tydrin—her boyfriend, her lover, the man aiding and abetting her?

She pursed her lips. All right. A big fat no to that last option. As far as titles went, it sucked. Was way too long as well. Nowhere near fun to explain to his pack either. Besides, *boyfriend* made her go all warm and fuzzy inside, ringing truer than anything else in a very long time.

Hands sliding down to her waist, Tydrin tipped his chin. "Ready?"

"Good to go," she said, lying through her teeth.

Approval sparked in his eyes. "There's my lass."

Giving her no chance to rethink her answer, he spun her around. Wood paneling whirled past. The walls blurred. Her feet caught on fancy rug fringe, making her trip and tilt sideways.

With a grumble curse, Ivy regained her equilibrium, but it too late. Embarrassed reared its ugly head and...

Wonderful.

Just perfect.

Exactly what she hoped to avoid—making a fool of herself, and a terrible first impression, right out of the gate.

Hands on her hips, Tydrin steadied her.

The room righted.

Her gaze landed on Wallaig. Surprise thumped on her. Her eyes widened and...holy crap. The guy was huge. A ginger-haired giant, tall, muscular, a lethal looking nightmare. One that screamed 'come closer, my pretty, so I can kill you.'

Tydrin walked her forward, toward the guy doing a fantastic impression of a serial killer.

Her footsteps slowed to a crawl. She squeezed his forearm to get his attention.

"Donnae let the size of him fool you, Ivy." Back in tow-her-behind-him mode, Tydrin pulled her around the end of a couch. "He'd never hurt a female."

Wallaig scowled. "Yer such a brat, Ty...ruining my fun."

"Since when do you have fun?"

"Every time I beat the snot out of you."

Tydrin scoffed. "That hasn't happened since I was a fledgling."

"Ah, the good old days," Wallaig said, fierce expression giving way to longing. "Such wonderful memories."

Eyes twinkling, Tydrin winked at her.

Ivy smiled against her will. How did he do that? Despite her nerves—and his relentless pace across the room—she found him way too charming. Lethal in his appeal. So frigging handsome, Ivy grumbled in resignation and gave up the fight. It was going to be all right. Perfectly okay. Tydrin had everything under control—her, himself, Wallaig and his nasty killer vibe too.

No reason to worry.

Or turn tail and run.

No matter how uneasy Wallaig made her, she trusted Tydrin to keep her safe and know who presented a real threat. And Wallaig? No matter how fierce the guy looked, he didn't make the cut.

The realization struck like a lightning bolt.

Sparks flew inside her head as the truth zapped her. Crazy fast. Unbelievability dangerous, but...she trusted Tydrin. Really *trusted* him.

She'd known she liked him—might even love him —but trust? Real put her life in his hands without years of data-driven proof *trust*? Her reaction was unprecedented. She liked data. Enjoyed the certainty of numbers and things she could see, but...*this*. The believe she could rely on Tydrin for anything—in all situations, scary or not—shook her foundations, pushing shock through her veins.

Ivy drew a shallow breath. The connection she felt with him was beyond strange. When had it happened—when he rescued her at the cemetery, during the midnight flight and the healing that came afterward...or was it after she woken up in his arms? She bit the inside of her bottom lip. The slow weave of magic explained some of it. The beauty of Tydrin did the rest, ticking off boxes she hadn't known existed before she met him. Which meant each one of her questions applied. Held sway. Pointed the way forward even as she struggled to understand his effect on her.

She must put away her doubts.

If she was going to trust him, she needed to go all the way. Hand Tydrin the reins and allow him to lead.

Stopping in front of his friend, Tydrin drew her against his side. "Wallaig, meet Ivy. Ivy meet the arsehole I've the misfortune tae call brother."

Angling his chin, Wallaig nodded at her. Hazel eyes bore into hers and—

Ivy frowned. Huh. Weird. His eyes all wrong.

Mere pinpoints, his pupils narrowed into vertical slits, slicing through golden-brown. A moment passed. Understanding struck. She opened her mouth before her brain told her to shut up. "You're blind."

Red brows popped up in surprise. "Observant, arenae you, lass?"

Ivy cringed. Stupid, stupid mouth. Hurrah for social awkwardness. And interminable pauses. She'd done it again, speaking without first allowing her brain to vet the contents.

Her hand flew up to cover her mouth. "Crap. I'm sorry. I shouldn't have mentioned—"

"Why not?" Wallaig shrugged. Muscles reacted to the shift, bunching under his T-shirt and over wide shoulders to ripple down his biceps. "'Tis naught more than the truth. I'd rather have your honesty than the alternative."

"The alternative?" Ivy asked, parroting him like an idiot.

"You pussy-footing around the fact I cannae see. Bugs the shite out of me when people do that." His gaze moved over her face. His regard intensified, giving Ivy the idea he could actually see her, then glanced at Tydrin. "With your permission."

"Make it quick, Wallaig," Tydrin said, moving behind her. His heat pressed against her back, warming her through as he set his hands on her waist. "I will never again permit you tae touch her."

"Understood."

Attention bouncing between the two men, Ivy tensed. "What—"

"Be still, *Talmina*," Wallaig said, stepping within arm's reach. "And know I will not hurt you. I wish tae see you, naught more."

*See her.* What in God's name did that mean?

The question buffeted her mind.

Wallaig raised his hands.

With a full body flinch, Ivy tried to back away.

Acting like a wall at her back, Tydrin tightened his grip and stopped her retreat. He murmured a reassurance. His friend touched her face. A wide palm found her jaw, held her still, then drifted up to explore her features. Butterfly touches across her cheekbones and down her nose. Calloused fingertips following the curves of her eyebrows. A gentle swipe against the thick fringe of eyelashes.

Ivy closed her eyes, struggling to be patient. She didn't like his hands on her. She didn't want to be touched by anyone but Tydrin. For all his gentleness, Wallaig's touch felt odd. Unsafe. Completely wrong.

Keeping each stroke light, he brushed his hands over her hair, smoothing the long strands from her temples, then moved down to trace the shells of her ears, *seeing* her the only way a blind man could.

"Enough," Tydrin growled, breaking the moment.

Ivy exhaled in relief.

"Verra pretty. Powerful energy." Dropping his hands, Wallaig stepped away. "You're a lucky bastard, Tydrin."

"I know." Tydrin kissed the top of her head.

A door creaked open behind Wallaig.

A tall, dark haired man stepped over the threshold. Nearly colorless, his pale violet eyes moved over her before he raised a brow. "Has she been seen?"

"She has, Cyprus." The corners of his mouth tipped up, Wallaig patted her shoulder and turned toward the new comer. "I like her. She's got a brilliant mind, set opinions too. Courage enough tae deal with the likes of Tydrin and all his bullshite, for certain."

Tydrin muttered something obscene.

Cyprus grinned. "Good news."

She scowled at Wallaig. "You do realize I'm standing right here?"

"Told you," Wallaig said, amusement in his tone. "A strong female. A true HE."

*A HE?* Another term she didn't recognize.

Ivy opened her mouth to ask for an explanation.

Tydrin tucked her under his arm, waylaying her question, prompting naughty thoughts and needy tingles. "Ivy, my older brother, Cyprus— commander of our pack."

"Nice to meet you." Awesome. A polite reply. She was getting the hang of it, climbing out of social ineptitude into the world of the well-mannered.

"Welcome, lass." With a nod, Cyprus tipped his head toward the door behind him. "Now, if you're all done here, 'tis time tae eat."

Wallaig perked up. "Is Rannock cooking?"

"Aye."

"Thank God." Eagerness winged across Tydrin's face.

Ivy raised a brow. "Rannock?"

"Another member of our pack," Tydrin said. "Wicked good in the kitchen. Of all of us, he prepares the best meals."

"How many of you are there?"

"Seven total, *Talmina*." Turning on his heel, Wallaig beat feet toward the kitchen. And holy crap. For a blind guy, he moved fast, without a hint of hesitation. "Levin and Kruger are flying in from the mountain lair. You'll meet them later. And Vyroth is—"

"Who the hell knows," Cyprus said, looking pissed off as he trailed behind his friend.

Taking her hand, Tydrin followed his brother. "Still no word?"

Cyprus shook his head.

A worried light entered Tydrin's eyes.

Ivy watched the exchange. Interesting. A secret along with a missing member of their pack. A state of affairs that clearly bothered both men. She made a mental note to ask Tydrin about it later. Who knew? She might be able to help. Give her a computer and everyone became traceable. Just a few key strokes away. Fair game on the world wide web.

Vyroth included.

Most people never thought about covering their cyber tracks. Or if they did, never well enough to fool her. A fact she was counting on the second Tydrin provided the equipment she needed to hunt her slime ball of an ex-boss and put Worth behind bars, where he belonged.

## 11

ARM SLUNG ACROSS the back of Ivy's chair, Tydrin watched his mate interact with his brothers-in-arms. First meal of the day decimated, the detritus of empty platters and cleaned plates in front of them, his packmates kicked back around the kitchen table. Same mealtime dynamic. No deviation in routine. All of his brothers relaxed like usual, acting as though sharing a meal with a female was no big deal. As though it happened every day, and Ivy hadn't sent shockwaves through the lair.

Tydrin appreciated the effort.

Loved his packmates all the more for attempting to put her at ease.

Especially since his female was anything but relaxed.

Nervous, unsure of herself, Ivy had spent the most of meal watching, and saying little. Seeing her struggle cracked him wide open. He disliked her uncertainty, and the fact she felt pressure to be perfect.

Plugged into her bio-energy, he read her without effort. She wanted to fit in. She needed to be accepted by his pack. She longed to make him proud.

Tydrin shifted in his seat.

Decades old, the wooden chair creaked beneath his bulk. Goddess help him. If only Ivy understood how proud she made him. He appreciated her desire to be accepted, understood the drive, wanted to make the transition from her world into his easier, but... shite. He didn't know how. All he could do was stay close and lend his support.

His quiet reassurance moved the dial, but not enough.

No matter what he did, she remained tense, never creating into comfortable. Fidgeting in her chair. Picking at her food. So afraid to make a mistake and say the wrong thing, it ruined her appetite. The moment she'd entered the kitchen, every move she made became calculated. Careful movements. Watchful pauses. Setting the utensils just so, adjusting and readjusting the plates on the tabletop, folding the napkins into perfect triangles...trying to do everything right.

His packmates pretended to ignore her tension. Carried on as they always did—telling stories, ribbing each other, jostling for position around the kitchen island, treating Ivy as though she was, and had always been, a permanent fixture inside the Scottish lair.

A deliberate strategy.

A brilliant one designed to send a clear message to his mate—she belonged. No need to be perfect or fear saying the wrong thing. She was welcome. She was home. No questions asked. No need to examine the premise. Just straight up respect for her and the nexus each male sensed growing between her and Tydrin.

A bond Ivy didn't yet comprehend.

Understandable.

To be expected.

She was new to Dragonkind. Didn't understand energy-fuse or what happened when a male's dragon half fixated on a female. The second the mating bond took hold, the dominos fell, cascading from immediate attraction into deep devotion.

No need to dig further or wonder about the outcome.

His need for her strengthened by the hour, making him yearn to claim her in the way of his kind. Tydrin wanted it all—the ceremony in front of his brothers, the ancient words spoken between mates, the mating mark that would forever proclaim her as his, and him as hers.

Nudging him under the table with his boot, Cyprus fired up mind-speak. *"Simmer down, Ty."*

*"I'm impatient."*

*"Understandable. She's an extraordinary female, but—"*

*"I know."* Shifting in his chair, he half-listened to the argument brewing between Ivy and Wallaig. *"Rushing her willnae work."*

*"Giver her time tae adjust. Let energy-fuse work and the connection deepen. You'll have what you need in the end."*

He hoped so.

Nothing in life was certain. The universe made no guarantees, and given Ivy's battle with the US government, the future seemed even less uncertain.

Cyprus tapped him again.

Tydrin tipped his chin in acknowledgement, then turned his attention back to the conversation. He caught the tail end of Wallaig's statement. His mouth curved. Christ. His packmate was in fine form tonight. Smart, a skilled conversationalist, the oldest, most experienced member of the Scottish pack, the male knew how what he was doing. Mostly pissing Ivy off, but...

Tydrin clenched his teeth to keep from smiling.

His brother was wily, straight up sharp, taking an opposing viewpoint, prompting a response, drawing Ivy out of her self-imposed shell.

Like magic, Wallaig's plan worked.

Provoked by his opinion, Ivy's uncertainty faded. She lost her shyness. A look of consternation on her face, she frowned as Wallaig argued some idiotic point of view. Rattling off a bunch of statistics, his packmate watched her with growing enjoyment, propping up his side of the discussion, trying to get a rise out of—

"That's a bunch of BS," Ivy said, scowling at Wallaig.

Bingo.

Target acquired.

Wallaig had struck gold, pushing Ivy into abandoning all caution.

"It's true enough," Wallaig insisted, provoking her on purpose. A smile playing at the corners of his mouth, the male pushed, defending a position he didn't believe, but...shite. His brother-in-arms enjoyed a good squabble. The more heated it got, the better Wallaig liked it. "Look at the data, lass. Numbers donnae lie."

"Total crap." Ivy's eyes narrowed on him. "You need to give your head a shake."

"Or better yet, have one of us bashed it in," Tydrin murmured, amused by the male's antics.

"I'd like tae see you try, laddie." Raising a ginger brow, Wallaig challenged him with a look, then frowned at him for interrupting his supercharged exchange with Ivy. "Shite. I'd have tae be blind *and* deaf tae not see you coming."

Cyprus snorted.

Rannock chuckled.

Kruger rolled his eyes.

Cool as the ice dragon he embodied, Levin stayed silent, but shook his head.

Crossing his booted feet under the table, Tydrin sat back and waited. Ivy wasn't a pushover. She was brilliant, her sharp intellect in constant motion as she examined all the angles. Something Wallaig was about to find out...the hard way.

"That data is skewed." Leaving forward in her chair, Ivy pointed at the tabletop. "You're just saying that cuz you're a guy. If women were given the same opportunities as men—fair hiring practices, equitable pay and equal treatment in tech industries—we'd kick ass and the statistics would shift."

Leaving back in his chair, Wallaig crossed his arms over his chest. "So it's discrimination?"

"Absolutely. You know how many women want to go into tech, but are discouraged by parents, teachers, guidance counselors, or just...you know, the over-arching, archaic attitudes of societal norms? Have you any idea how many women apply for jobs in the tech industry every year?" she asked, throwing down her napkin, no longer worried about perfectly folded corners.

Wallaig shrugged, egging her on.

Agitated, warming to the subject, she shoved her plate away. "Thousands. Like seriously...*thousands of women*. And do you know how many actually get jobs?"

Wallaig shook his head.

"Not nearly enough. It's almost a hundred men to one woman."

"Mayhap, females donnae possess enough fortitude for the tech industry."

"Maybe, I need to stab you with my fork."

Enjoying her reaction, his brother smiled. "You're a feisty bit of baggage, arena you?"

Grabbing a discarded chicken bone off her plate, Ivy tossed it across the table at Wallaig. The reminisce of her supper smacked into the chest of his chest, smearing sauce on his shirt.

Unable to contain his amusement, Tydrin huffed.

Her focus snapped in his direction. "What's the protocol?"

Holding his gaze, Tydrin raised a brow. "Protocol?"

"Dragon protocol," she said, gesturing to Wallaig. "Am I allowed to stab him or not?"

"Calm, *talmina*," Wallaig murmured, calling her *little one* in Dragonese, laughter in his tone. "I'm just messing with you."

She blinked. "Come again?"

"I'm pulling your leg, lass."

"As in...teasing me."

"Aye."

She pursed her lips. "I still have the urge to stab you."

Wiping BBQ sauce off his t-shirt, Wallaig tossed the bone onto his plate. "You've got agree, there is some truth tae what I said."

Ivy frowned. "Wallaig—"

"Males and females are different, Ivy. Why would anyone want us to be the same? The challenges we face require different skill sets, different strengths and weaknesses, different ways of viewing the world, new approaches to tackling problems that have plagued us for years. The difference between the sexes isnae a bad thing, lass. We need differing points of view tae succeed, tae find better ways forward, but then..." Palming his empty glass, Wallaig rattled the ice against the crystal. "The human view has always been fucked up. Your kind have it backwards. Have from the beginning."

"Backwards?"

"Ivy—females rule the world. Always have, in one way or another. Dragonkind understands how important you are tae us. We would never clip your wings... or get in your way. Skill is skill—man, woman—who gives a fuck where and who it comes from?"

"CEOs, apparently," Ivy said, sitting back in her chair. "You like messing with people, don't you?"

"Spirited argument, lass. Most fun I've had in a while. Besides..." Putting his glass down, Wallaig motioned to his eyes. "I cannae read. I like learning new things, collecting differing opinions, and arguing with smart females helps pass the time."

"Ever heard of audiobooks?" she asked, treating him to a pointed look. "Seriously, Wallaig. We need to get you some."

Wallaig grinned. "Healthier for me in the long run."

"Well, it would keep me from maiming you."

The males around the table laughed.

Scooting his chair back, Tydrin stood and reached for his mate. Soft skin slid against his rougher palm. Her hand in his, he tugged her to her feet. "Time to go, lovely. I've got something tae show you."

Lacing her fingers through his, she followed him around table.

He tipped his chin at his brothers. "Later, lads."

Getting a round of "ayes", leaving his brother-in-arms to clean up the kitchen, he pulled Ivy out the door, across the great room and up a set of stairs. At the top, he crossed the circular landing. Elevator to the Dragon's Horn—the pub he owned with his brothers —above ground to his right. Double wide corridor to his left. He veered left, towing his mate toward the Hub, a room inside the lair he knew she'd appreciate.

Walking past the gym kitted out with the best money could buy, he strode past the infirmary full of medical supplies and headed for the end of the hall. Rough white-washed granite walls streamed passed. His footfalls echoed on the polished concrete floors. Light globes reacted to displaced air, bobbing like jellyfish against fifteen-foot ceilings.

"This is cool. Pretty plain, though. You need something on the walls," she said, looking around. "Not art from a gallery, exactly. I think...maybe...professional graffiti would suit the lair better."

Graffiti?

Tydrin's mouth curved. "If you can get Cyprus tae agree, have at it, Ivy."

"Terrific," she muttered, pursing her lips. "Like I'm ever going to have *that* conversation with your badass brother."

Enjoying her wit, approaching the double doors at the end of the corridor, Tydrin squeezed her hand. "Ready?"

"For the computer you promised me?"

Smart lass. His female didn't miss much. And he didn't explain.

With a murmur, he unleashed his magic. Heat swirled down the corridor in front of him. The electronic keypad beeped. Double deadbolts flicked open. He turned the handle with his mind and, with a mental push, opened one of the heavy steel doors.

Motion detectors went live.

Lights inside the room powered up, illuminating the back wall.

Releasing her hand, Tydrin sidestepped, allowing Ivy to enter the Hub first.

His female sucked in a sharp breath.

"Computer central, Ivy," he murmured, watching wonder suffuse her face.

She opened her mouth. Close it again.

Shocked speechless, she held his gaze a moment, then headed straight for desk. Built in a half circle, the gleaming black top faced a bank of wall-mounted flat screen monitors. Dark now, but not for long as Ivy crouch to check out the hardware beneath the desk.

"Holy crap," she whispered, examining the state-of-the-art computer system. "This is serious tech, Tydrin. Most people don't even know this stuff exists. How did you get your hands on it?"

He shrugged. "Ask Levin."

"Does he know how to use it?"

"Not really," he said, watching her excitement grow as she checked out the system Levin installed over a year ago. Why? Tydrin didn't know. No one knew how to operate any of the equipment locked behind steel doors and miles of granite. "But if you want it, Ivy, the Hub is yours."

Pushing to her feet, she slid her hand over the back of the fancy office chair. "Mine?"

"Aye. Every bit of it."

"The damage I could do," she whispered, staring at him. "All the good I could do from here."

Standing just inside the door, not knowing how to react, he stared back. Silence invaded the room, stretching between them. His full of uncertainty. Hers filled with something akin to wonder.

A furrow between her brows, she stood unmoving in the center of the room. A second passed. Then another. On the third, she drew in an unsteady breath and...

Launched herself at him.

He stepped into her flight path, catching her mid-jump as she leapt up. His arms came around her. Legs wrapped around his waist, she murmured his name as her mouth touched down on his.

Hands buried in his hair, she nibbled on his bottom lip. "This room ever been christened?"

Holding her tight, he accepted her kiss and shook his head.

"About time, don't you think?"

Absolutely.

No time like the present.

With Ivy in his arms, getting down and dirty anywhere sounded like a fantastic idea.

"Clothes off," she whispered a second before she invaded his mouth.

Addicted to the feel of her, Tydrin didn't object...or waste any time.

With a mental command, he slammed the door closed behind him, flipped the locks, and got down to business—stripping her bare, tasting her deep, pleasuring her hard as he took her against the back wall, powering into her slick heat, making her moan in front of a powerful computer that now belonged to her, just like him.

## 12

THE FAST CLICK of computer keys broke through the quiet. The flash of text, black on white, flashed across the large screens mounted on the wall. Fingers flying over the keyboard, Ivy shifted her hand position. Her wrists slid across the smooth marble desktop. Veins of gold spread across the black surface, drawing crooked lines on expressive stone.

Ivy didn't notice.

Seated in the curve of her new desk, butt planted in the ergonomic chair, she tapped the down arrow, scrolled through each page, hunting for the last piece in her puzzle.

The tidbit was here...somewhere.

All she needed to do was find it.

Eyes glued to the center screen, she indulged in a sip of coffee. The rich hazelnut flavor rolled over her tongue. Ivy hummed in approval. Just the way she liked it. Java Joe at its finest, delivered by Tydrin just minutes ago in the biggest mug she'd even seen.

Her mouth curved around the ceramic rim.

She took another sip.

God love the man. He was all kinds of wonderful.

Awesomeness squared. Nah. Up that number, please. Make it to the power of a hundred.

And no wonder.

After three weeks with him, she still couldn't quantify his thoughtfulness. Ivy sighed as happiness filtered through her. Twenty-one days with Tydrin would never be enough. She recognized the all-encompassing truth the first day. Now she wanted more and needed everything—his heart, his home, a new life with a pack of Dragonkind guys who liked to keep her guessing.

Ivy pressed the down key, working her way through more documents. Tydrin, she understood. The other guys? Not so much. At least, not yet. Give her time and she'd tag them all. Have their numbers. Be able to understand how each one ticked, but well... she paused, fingers hovering over the keyboard...so far that hadn't happened. The internal workings of each warrior still eluded her.

Which was weird.

She might not be great in social situations, but she knew how to read people. Finding out what made her targets tick was an essential part of her job. Understanding individual quirks, after all, lead to easier hacks. The more she knew about a person, the easier it became to guess passwords and infiltrate emails. With so much practice getting into other people's heads, she should be able to figure out Tydrin's pack-mates. Lickety spilt fast—she frowned—right?

Pursing her lips, Ivy nodded.

Sure. Absolutely. No question about it.

Staring unseeing at the screen, she thought it through. A number of adjectives for the guys sprang to mind. Her eyes narrowed as her mind whirled, churning out facts, classifying data, ordering the sum total into a complete list. All right, here went nothing...

Characteristic number one of pack mentality—hardcore warrior vibe with violent tendencies. Yup. Without a doubt. Put that at the top the list. Ivy nibbled on her lip as she pictured Tydrin in dragon form—and the crazy midnight flight he'd taken her on last night.

At first, she'd been freaked out. Five minutes in, she'd been enthralled. Totally in love with dragon flight and her secure seat on Tydrin's back. Add in the other warriors flying in fighting formation around him—wings spread wide, scales of different shades glinting in the moonlight, vapor trails spiraling off spiked tails—and the experience had gone from incredible to majestic.

And all that before dragon combat training began.

Ivy shook her head.

Man oh man, talk about intense. Deadly too. The US military and their arsenal of heat seeking missiles couldn't compete with Tydrin's pack. Or the huge, crazy-ass fireballs the group let fly...you know...just for *fun*.

Totally bizarre. Super entertaining to watch from a safe distance.

Leaning back in her chair, Ivy grinned at her tacky mug. Again. She wanted to go flying *again*. Tonight. Tomorrow night. Every night after that too.

She loved soaring in open skies—the speed of dragon flight, the hot burn of adrenaline in her veins, the idea she was now a part of something specular, the newest member of a Dragonkind pack with a secret to keep and a family to protect. With a wary chuckle, she fired up numbers two, three and four on her list—

watchful and overprotective with shades of completely exasperating.

She sighed.

Uh-huh. Absolutely. Those items deserved special mention. Stick a big fat asterisk beside each one.

The constant babying—or spoiling, as each warrior preferred to call it—chaffed her independent nature. She couldn't twitch without one of the guys noticing. Or go anywhere without an escort.

The group had made that clear, laying down the law her first night inside the lair.

Not a bad thing as far as precautions went. She agreed with the basic principle. At least, for now.

With the FBI still hunting her, a certain amount of caution should be observed. But honestly, Tydrin needed to loosen the reins a bit. An hour—maybe two —every day would do the trick. Not long enough for him to worry, but enough time for her to get some sun on her face while she exploded the shops close to the Dragon's Horn.

Ivy glanced at the clock tick-tick-tocking, keeping perfect time on the back wall.

Five oh five on the nose.

Twenty minutes to sundown.

Her gaze flicked around the Hub—a space she'd made her own. Warm wood paneling installed over cold concrete walls. A deep-seated couch and a couple comfortable armchairs with soft throw pillows stationed at the back of the room. A couple of plush area rugs strewn across the floor, reflecting the same turquoise color painted on the ceiling. Perfection wrapped up in one kick-ass computer room. And now, all hers. Even so—

Her attention swung to the door.

Maybe she should go out to the courtyard for a

while. Sit by the creepy snake fountain. Soak up some rays. Relax a bit and return to hunting for proof of Worth's guilt after supper.

Temptation urged her to get up and go.

The need to reclaim her life kept her seated.

It wouldn't be long now. Another hour. Two at most, and she'd find what she needed to nail her ex-boss. Foolish to hope so hard? Perhaps, but Ivy didn't think so. With her specialized decryption software up and running and the trapdoors she'd dropped into the NSA's firewall, she was close. So very close to catching the rat, she could almost taste it.

Taking another sip of Joe, she set her mug down and continued to hunt. Classified documents flew past on screen. One caught her attention. Ivy paused the scroll-down. Reading rapid fire, she scanned each line. Fisting her hand, she thumped the top of her desk.

Pencils sitting in a glass jar jumped, bumping across black marble.

The clink cracked through the quiet as she growled in satisfaction. Finally. About frigging time. After weeks of searching—of playing hide and seek on the dark net while infiltrating INP Securities' databases—she'd hit pay dirt and—

Eureka!

There it was. The final document. The last nail in Worth's coffin.

"Got you." Ivy typed in a quick command. The light on her computer drive flickered. Her super computer whined and...

Fantastic.

File saved.

Shoving her keyboard away, she rolled her shoulders. Stiff muscles stretched, sending painful prickles down her spine. Discomfort threatened to ruin the mood. She ignored it and, ejecting the drive, pulled it from the USB port.

Staring at her salvation, she curled her hand around the memory stick. "I *got* you, you worthless bastard."

Her words bounced around her office.

Ivy sat stunned for a moment. She'd done it. *Really done it.* Gamed the system. Beat Worth at his own game. Unearthed the proof that would sink him and set her free.

Emotion clogged her throat. The desire to tell Tydrin popped her to her feet. Her running shoes squeaked against the polished concrete floor. The chair rolled back, wheels squealing in protest as she headed toward the door.

She needed to see him. Right now. Wanted to share the good news, celebrate her triumph and ask for a hug. Only his arms would do. No other man settled and soothed her the way he did, and as she picked up the pace, speed walking the door, Ivy knew no one else ever would.

Wood paneling blurred in her periphery.

Sliding to a stop, she palmed the door handle and yanked. Hinges opened with a quiet hiss. Feet doing double time, she jogged down the hall, through the circular landing, past the elevator, down the stairs into the common area. Stained glass flashed above her head as she scanned the room.

Empty.

Not a soul in sight.

Crap. Not what she wanted to see at the moment. Maybe Tydrin was upstairs in the pub, working the bar, serving the latest round of human patrons.

Rounding a long couch, she skirted a quadruplet of armchairs. The murmur of male voices reached her.

Her head snapped toward a pair of double doors. The timbre of Tydrin's baritone drifted from the kitchen. Ivy's mouth curved. Perfect. She should've expected it. Creatures of habit, the warriors always gathered around the island this time each day.

Feeling as though she'd burst if she didn't tell Tydrin her news soon, she crossed the ocean of Persian rugs, planted her palms against wood, and pushed one of the swinging doors open. She paused to get the lay of the land. Her eyes went to work, providing a quick snapshot. Everyone home, all the guys present and accounted for.

Wide backs to her, Wallaig, Levin and Kruger sat on high stools at the kitchen island, elbows planted on the stone countertop, their gazes fixed on Cyprus. Standing in front of the six burner stove, Rannock angled his head, listening intently as he stirred something. And Cyprus and Tydrin? The brothers sat to one side, facing off across the glossy surface of a polished cherry wood table.

She opened her mouth to greet the pack.

The tension in the room registered.

She swallowed her hello as the current of unease crackled like electricity, making the fine hairs on her nape stand on end. Not knowing what to do, Ivy stood still and ran her gaze over Tydrin.

Intuition spiked.

The connection she shared with him flared, tuning her into his emotional state.

She turned the dial, increasing her ability to read him and...oh, no. Not good. Worried. Stressed. Upset about something. She frowned at the back of his head. He was afraid for someone. So tense she sensed the flex and claw of his concern, and in that moment knew whatever bothered him had to do with her.

Dread coiled in the pit of her stomach.

Something was about to go wrong—very, very *wrong*.

Focused on Tydrin, she stepped further into the room. The wooden door closed behind her with a soft whoosh and—

"There's no easy way, Ty." Forearms folded on the tabletop, pale eyes fixed on his brother, Cyprus leaned in. "You need tae tell Ivy now—tonight. The longer you leave it, the more difficult it will become."

A chill raced down her spine. "Tell me what?"

With muttered curses, the warriors swung around to face her. The abrupt shift pushed chairs across the tiled floor. Wooden legs screeched against ceramic, making the trio at the island cringe.

"Bloody hell." Shoving away from the table, Tydrin pushed to his feet. Head bowed, shoulders hunched, he lifted his chin to look at her. His fierce expression softened as he met her gaze. "Ivy-mine."

"You can do this, Tydrin," Cyprus said, soft tone full of encouragement. "Tell her."

"What's going on?" Curiosity collided with fear, closing her throat. Swallowing hard, Ivy drew a full breath. "Did I do something wrong?"

Blond hair glinting beneath halogens, Levin shook his head.

Turning on the stool, black-eyes narrowed, Kruger glowered at Tydrin.

"No chance in hell," Rannock growled and, raising his huge hand, slammed a wooden spoon against the pot edge. The nasty clang echoed through the kitchen, banging off walnut cabinetry. "Bugger it, Tydrin. Pull your head out of your arse, will yah?"

Wallaig scowled. "Nay, *talmina*, you dinnae do anything wrong."

"Tydrin?" she asked, ignoring the trio at the island.

"I need tae tell you something, lovely," Tydrin said, his unease so powerful Ivy shivered. The internal tremor shook her, raising instinct to new levels. Tydrin might not know it yet, but he needed her. His pain became hers, throbbing in her veins, curling around her rib cage, making her want to hug him hard and never let go. "I donnae know how tae...I cannae..."

As he trailed off, Ivy stepped toward him.

Tydrin backed away.

Sidestepping, he used the chair as a barrier and, holding her gaze, shook his head. His actions spoke louder than words. He didn't want her to approach. With an unspoken demand, he asked for distance, rejecting the comfort of her touch and—

A nasty suspicion took hold.

She drew in a shaky breath. Whatever he wanted to say was bad. Worse than terrible. Most likely catastrophic given his expression. She read the warning in his eyes and felt the truth in her bones. Her hand tightened around the memory stick. Plastic bit into her palm. She ignored the pain as another sort shot through her.

Agony pierced her breastbone, heading straight for her heart.

Ivy absorbed the blow, fighting to keep from doubling over. Ah, God. Someone please put her out of her misery. She wouldn't survive the fallout. It didn't matter that she'd known it was too good to be true. Too good last—that he'd eventually change his mind and ask her to leave. The law of averages didn't lie. Neither did social ineptitude, a distinctly unlovable quality and...

Heaven help her.

She wasn't ready. Didn't want to let him go or leave

the lair. Not yet. Or ever. But as sure as she stood staring at him, Ivy knew what he wanted to say.

It was over.

He was done.

The man she loved intended to call it quits. Three weeks with her had been enough. He didn't desire her anymore.

The realization struck with the force of a nuclear bomb, rocking her foundation. A tremor rumbled through her. Ivy reached for courage, struggling not to breakdown. But as her heart broke and tears pooled in her eyes, Ivy knew she wouldn't make it. Devastation did that to a girl, destroying her willpower when she needed it most.

**13**

---

**D**READ MADE Tydrin's heart pound harder. The chaotic beat echoed in his veins before travelling to his head. Now he couldn't hear much of anything. Only one thought registered. He didn't want to tell her. He wanted to hide his crime instead. Bury the facts deep. Cover up his sins and never look back. It would be so easy to do—ignore his conscience, forget about the past, convince himself Ivy didn't need to know.

Twenty years was a long time. Practically ancient history.

Maybe that's the way it needed to stay—hidden.

An excellent strategy.

The perfect counter argument to the truth—Tydrin blew out a long breath—and a really bad idea. He knew it deep down. Could see all the pitfalls, each and every place his principles would trip him up. But as he held Ivy's gaze, fear collided with temptation, urging him to forsake right, accept wrong, and keep her in the dark. Silence, after all, was sometimes the better part of valor. And some secrets were meant to be kept.

Indecision running riot, he waffled another moment.

Tydrin flexed his hands. Open. Closed. Curl and retreat. The small movement didn't help him make a decision. No question he could pull it off—lie, cheat and steal as long as he got to keep her.

A dirty move? Absolutely.

Unscrupulous with an extra helping of nasty? Without a doubt.

No excuse for it either way. And yet, as seconds ticked past and the silence lengthened into uncomfortable, the idea consumed him, providing hope and newfound possibility. A lot less future pain too, 'cause sure as shite, the instant Ivy learned the truth, she'd leave him.

Turn tail, run and never look back.

But not before he saw horror bloom in her eyes.

She'd never look at him the same way. Not with love and acceptance. Never again with the lust-filled expression he adored seeing on her face. Her desire for him would die a swift death. Poof, gone, over in an instant. Ivy might even accuse him of being a monster once the truth came out. She'd no doubt yell and cry, call him the worst sort of bastard for taking what he wanted— nay, needed, craved, couldn't live without—before coming clean and telling her the truth.

Tydrin closed his eyes.

He wanted to turn back time. Be a better male and make different choices. Waylay the fireball. Change its course across the night sky. Snuff out the explosion and save her parents' lives.

Regret rose, threatening to choke him.

Bloody hell, one mistake. One millisecond fraught with miscalculation. A moment of misjudgment—and the loss of his temper—had led to this...him standing in his kitchen about to mislead his mate. His love. The only female he would never be able to live without and—

Shite. Stupid conscience. He couldn't go through with it.

A Dragonkind male never lied to his mate. For any reason. And if he chose to now, the knowledge would eat him alive. Ivy deserved better from him. His female deserved his all. Every bit of his love and devotion. All his blood, sweat and focus. But more than anything, she needed his honesty.

Building a life with her based on a lie would ruin them both in the end. His brother was right. No matter how great the pain—or what the risk—he must tell her the truth.

"Tydrin?" Framed by the double doors, she met his gaze.

The plea in her eyes almost killed him. Fuck. He was a first class fool. A real bastard for increasing her fear by allowing the silence to continue. He should be over there, soothing her uncertainty, softening the blow the truth would deliver. He told himself to move. His feet refused to leave the floor. He stared at her instead, heart hurting, voice silenced, keenly aware he didn't deserve to hold her.

Not right now. No doubt never again.

Releasing a shaky breath, Ivy took a step toward him. "I don't know what's going on, but talk to me. Please, just tell me."

"It's my fault, lovely," he said, finding his voice. "All my fault. I should've talked tae you sooner—on the very first day."

"About what?"

"Ivy, I need tae tell you something about the night your parents—"

"Oh, thank God." Relief replaced the fear in her eyes. Her hand flew up to cover her mouth. "Thank God."

Her outburst knocked him off balance.

What had she just said—*thank God*?

Confusion set up shop inside his head. Unable to adjust, he gaped at her. "Excuse me?"

Her eyes closed. The fringe of her eyelashes flickered as she raised her hands, tucked errant strands of hair behind her ears, then raised her chin. Ocean blue eyes met his, making his heart clench. "Sorry, I didn't mean to interrupt. I mean...I can see whatever you have to say is important but, I thought...I thought..."

As she trailed off, hunting for words, she swallowed.

Tydrin watched her throat work. His gaze strayed to the side of her neck, the place where her pulse beat the strongest. He loved that spot. Adored running his mouth over it until she moaned his name and he tasted her on his tongue—rich, sweet, perfect in every way.

The thought triggered another.

An image sped into his head, one of Ivy above him, hips moving, gorgeous breasts on display, the deluge of pleasure as she rode him. Desire slammed through him, readying his body, scrambling his mind, stealing more of his wits just as Ivy recovered hers.

Color swept back into her cheeks. Her lips tipped up at the corners.

Lust took another unwelcome leapt forward. His dragon half reacted, tightening muscles over his bones.

Tydrin clenched his teeth. Shite. Not good. Nowhere near advisable. He needed to keep his head in the game. The seriousness of the issue demanded it. So did he. Sex wasn't on the table. Hell, it shouldn't even be in the same room. The thought was practically blasphemous given the situation, so...aye. He flexed his hands. Right. No doubt at all. He needed to keep his head out of the gutter and the conversation on track. If only to retain his own sanity. Excellent. A plan worth sticking to and—

Ivy smiled at him.

His libido went into overdrive, darting in dangerous directions.

"You scared me," she said, pressing her hand to her chest. "I thought you were breaking up with me."

Surprise stopped him cold.

"What?" Surprise knocked him off stride. Again. Like always. Fuck. He was useless today. Every time she opened her mouth, he lost track of the conversation. Tydrin shook his head, trying to get his brain to work. "Bloody hell, lovely, why would you think such a—"

"Stupid thing?" Levin snorted, the sound full of disbelief. "Lass, you need your wee head examined."

His gaze snapped toward his meddling comrade.

Unrepentant as always, the mouthy jackoff raised a brow.

Tydrin glared at him.

Wallaig elbowed the idiot in the ribs, saving Tydrin a trip across the kitchen to beat the snot out of his friend. Levin grunted and, with a muttered "hey", rubbed the sore spot.

"Shut yer gob." Expression stern, Wallaig warned the younger male with a look. "Let the lad deal with his female."

Tydrin nodded his thanks.

"Donnae mention it," Wallaig said, unseeing hazel eyes still narrowed on Levin.

Switching his attention back to Ivy, Tydrin scowled at her. *Break up with her*? Where the hell had she gotten that idea? His female clearly didn't understand her value. Or how much he adored her. Needed her. Craved her. Didn't want to live without her...whatever. Throw in every desire-fueled word to describe his yearning for her, and it still wouldn't be enough. But the fact she doubted her importance to him? Completely unacceptable. A circumstance in need of change. Right now. Before he crossed the kitchen and paddled her behind—along with some sense into her —instead of saying what he wanted to say.

"I love you, Ivy," he said, handing her his heart without hesitation. It didn't matter that she would probably stomp on it later. She needed to know how much she meant to him. And that given half a chance, he would make her happy, give her everything, never allow her to want for a single thing for the rest of their lives. "You are my mate. My perfect match, mine tae hold for all eternity. I want tae marry you, not break up with you."

She blinked. "Really?"

The uncertainty in her voice did him in. Wrong shoved right out of the way, then threw it out the nearest window.

Tydrin swallowed a growl. Screw it. Consequences be damned. If he was to lose her tonight, he wanted to hold her one last time. Shoving the chair out of the way, he held out his hand. "Come here, lass."

She didn't hesitate.

Shoving something into her front pocket, Ivy took flight across the kitchen. Her shoes squeaked against the tile floor. Eyes full of tears, she slid into his embrace, bumping into him before settling against him. Tydrin closed his arms around her. The smell of heather and sweet mountain air—so familiar, all Ivy —enveloped him. He breathed deep, reveling in the scent of her skin, and sighed in relief.

Instant acceptance.

Unending respite.

Incredible connection.

He would never get enough of having her in his arms.

Holding her close, he cupped the back of her head. Soft strands of her hair caressed his palm. She snuggled in, arms around him, hands fisted in the back of his shirt, her heart beating next to his. "Listen closely, luv. Before we go any further—or you accept what I'm offering—I need tae tell you something important. Something that may change the way you feel about me."

Cheek nestled against his chest, she shook her head. "Impossible."

"Very possible, but it cannae be helped. I need tae tell you," he murmured against the top of her head. "Will you let me explain without interruption?"

She nodded.

Tydrin took a fortifying breath. The moment of truth had arrived. Now or never. Keep his secret or let her decide if she wanted him in the aftermath of confession.

His throat closed on the words that would seal his fate.

Determination spurred him forward, urging him to start talking. "I was there the night your parents died, Ivy. It was my fault. I killed them. I didn't mean tae. It was an accident. A horrible, awful accident, but the truth is—I caused their deaths."

Stillness descended, blanketing the room. His admission hung in the air. No one moved. Hell, he didn't even breathe as he waited for Ivy to react. To respond. To shove him away and start running.

A furrow appeared between her brows.

One second tumbled into more before she lifted her head. The warmth of her cheek left his chest. Fear cracked him wide open, making it hard to breath and—

Her gaze met his, then narrowed. "The hell you did, Tydrin."

Surprised by the conviction in her tone, Tydrin flinched. Christ. Was she truly that stubborn? So enamored of him she couldn't hear the truth?

He frowned. Maybe. Maybe not. Either way, it didn't matter. Her disbelief didn't change the facts. Accident or nay, he'd done what he'd *done*. She'd suffered in the aftermath. Now he must pay the price. Honor dictated the play. The need for honesty pushed the agenda. He was a warrior born and bred, strong enough to accept his culpability and admit to his crime. Freedom lay in climbing out of the guilt to take refuge in the truth. He needed her to accept it. Wanted her forgiveness too. Otherwise, he wouldn't stand a chance of keeping her in his life.

"'Tis the truth," he said, his throat so tight it hurt to talk. "I know you've no wish tae believe it, lass, but I am responsible. I lost control of a fireball too close tae town. It hit the knoll behind your parent's cottage. I snuffed out the flames, but an ember must've flared to life after I left and started a fire in the grass. The oil tank behind your house exploded and—"

"That's not what happened."

He opened his mouth to object.

Both hands flat on his chest, Ivy shook her head. "I can appreciate that's what you *think* happened, Tydrin, but it isn't. Didn't you read the Fire Inspector's report?"

Cyprus pushed away from the table. Chair legs scraped across limestone as he stood. "What report?"

"The one I hacked Scottish Fire and Rescue to read when I was thirteen."

"Thirteen?" Wooden spoon abandoned beside the stove, Rannock crossed his arms and leaned back against the countertop. "Bloody hell, lass. You're a wee felon."

Ivy shrugged. "My aunt refused to get the report. The Fire and Rescue Service refused to send it to me because I was a minor. Quickest thing to do was get it myself."

"Do you still have the report?" Cyprus asked.

"I can get it," Ivy said, without looking at his brother. Focused wholly on Tydrin, she slid her palm over his shoulder and down his arm. He shivered as she laced her fingers with his. "Come with me."

Feet rooted to the floor, he shook his head.

"Please, Tydrin." Holding his hand, she backed out of his embrace. His elbow straightened as she walked backward. Reaching the limit of his arm span, she held his hand in both of hers and tugged, pulling him off balance. "Let me show you."

The plea in her voice broke through his shock.

She tugged again.

His feet moved and he followed, allowing her to lead him out of the kitchen and across the common room. The doors swung closed behind him. Held tight by her gentle touch, he kept his eyes on her. The furniture didn't register as he walked past. Neither did the fancy rugs under his feet or the colorful dome above his head. His mind wasn't working right. He was lost, stunned by the inconceivable, mired in possibility, hoping so hard that Ivy was right he couldn't do a thing but let her lead.

Without breaking stride, she retraced her steps to the Hub. Wood paneling below a turquoise ceiling registered. She continued to walk. Tydrin followed as she drew him through the large space and stopped in alcove of her desk. "Stand right there. Don't move."

He didn't answer.

She gave him a reassuring squeeze and dropped his hand, leaving him to stand like an idiot behind her chair. He couldn't help it. The zombie act was the best he could manage under the circumstances. He'd assumed the blame. Carried the shame. Accepted his mistake and tried to make amends for twenty years.

Pressure built behind his eyes. Disbelief jabbed at him. How could this be? What Ivy said couldn't be true, but even as logic pressed the point, hope made a giant leap forward. Please, Goddess, let her be right. Let him be innocent—exonerated... whatever. The finer details didn't matter just as long as—

Ivy mumbled something.

The fast click of computer keys jolted through the quiet.

Tydrin snapped back to the present. His focus narrowed on his female.

Blue eyes on the center screen, Ivy leaned forward in her office chair. Fingers flying and expression fierce, she opened window after window, hacking databases, slipping through what she liked to call trapdoors, to find the file she wanted. Minutes passed. Tydrin counted off each second, afraid to breath, daring to hope, his chest so tight pain spiraled around his torso.

With a hum, Ivy brought a document forward on her screen. She pushed to her feet, turned to face him, then pointed to her chair. "Sit down and read that."

Her tone brooked no argument.

Despite his nervousness, Tydrin's mouth curved. Fierce wee sprite, wasn't she? Bossy bit of goods too. Even so, he refused to argue. He sat down instead. Springs groaned. Wheels squawked as he rolled forward, planted his elbows on the marble desktop, and started reading.

Seventeen paragraphs and nearly five pages later, he read the fire inspector's summery.

Incredulity slid like a dagger between his ribs.

Tydrin sucked in a quick breath. The words on the page blurred as his eyes teared and...bloody hell. That couldn't be right—could it? He scanned the last paragraph again, slower this time. Astonishment warred with acceptance. Pushing away from the desk, he sat unmoving, his attention glued to the document.

Ivy's hand slid over the nape of his neck.

The soft caress made his heart tremble. "I donnae understand. I was so sure. So—"

"Wrong, baby," she whispered, pushing her fingers into his hair. Freedom lived in her touch. In the gentle stroke of her hand and the love he sensed in her. "I've read that report over and over. Probably a hundred times, Tydrin. An explosion didn't kill them. My parents both died of smoke inhalation. An electrical fire started in the kitchen and..." Her voice hitched. His heart broke for her. "Mom and Dad died in their sleep, long before the fire reached them."

"Fuck," he said, starting at the fire inspector's signature at the bottom of the last page. "He even noted the crater of scorched earth in the backyard."

"Where your fireball hit."

"Aye."

"I always wondered about that spot—and what caused it." Moving to his shoulders, she massaged taut muscle, attacking his tension with her wee hands. "The burnt patch was too far from the house to have impacted the investigation. The inspector noted it anyway."

"Thorough bugger."

"Thank God. Because of him, you know the truth now."

"That I do, lovely. That I do," he said, voice soft with wonder.

Tears stung the corners of his eyes. Reaching out without looking, he shackled Ivy's wrist. A gentle tug. A quick twist of the chair, and she landed in his lap. She settled like a gift, tucking in, bringing him comfort, warming him as the past uncurled its ragged claws and finally let him go. Light invaded, cleansing his soul, chasing the darkness away, leaving him bright and shiny new.

Dipping his head, he brushed his mouth against hers. "Thank you, Ivy."

"You're welcome," she whispered, accepting him without hesitation. "You've tortured yourself for years haven't you, Tydrin?"

The question hung between them.

Throat gone tight, not knowing what to say, he kissed her again. She took it deeper, tangling their tongues, feeding him joy with each stroke. Drawing away, she rubbed her cheek against his and shifted in his lap.

leaned back in the chair.

She threw her leg over his hips and settled astride him, making his body jump. "That stops right now. I won't have it."

His hands found her hips. "Will you not?"

"No," she said, warning him with a no-nonsense look "I love you, Tydrin. I can't stand to see you hurting."

The words hit him chest level. His fingers flexed on her hips. Three little words. The ones he'd wanted to hear for what seemed like an eternity. "You love me?"

"I do. More than is sensible, I'm afraid."

"'Tis the first time you've said it."

"I was waiting for the right time. Today...here, right now, I think...qualifies."

"So it does," he said, his heart so full it threatened to overflow. "I love you, Ivy-mine. You are a gift I dinnae expect and donnae deserve, but I'm a greedy bastard. I'm taking you anyway. Marry me?"

"I should probably warn you." Excitement sparked in her eyes, then turned to mischief. "I want the fairy-tale—a princess dress, bouquets of wild roses, a midnight carriage ride through town and—"

"A thousand year old church with a grumpy priest and a choir of altar boys?"

Her mouth curved. "Perfect."

"Aye, it is," he murmured, smiling back. "Perfect in every way."

The *perfect* Dragonkind wedding.

Lavish. Beautiful. An event without equal.

Everything his female wanted and he needed to make her his.

Crazy, maybe, considering his kind, but he didn't care. Ivy had set her heart in his hands. He would hold it high and protect her always. And as she kissed him again and he saw to her needs, he thanked his lucky stars. His female surpassed all others. She was glory and light, spectacular in every way. And as he stripped her down and tasted her deep, he knew their union would be the stuff of legends, a fairytale in the making, a love without end.

## 14

OSLO, NORWAY – ONE MONTH LATER

B OOTS PLANTED on a cracked section of
sidewalk, Tydrin stared at the tall brick
building across the street. A secondhand book
store and a boutique coffee bar occupied the first floor.
Swanky apartments occupied the rest. Some residents
were still up, lights on, wandering around their flats in
ugly pajama's, but the shops, at least, were closed for
the night.

Thank Christ.

He didn't need anyone screwing with his plans.
Least of all a bunch of humans looking for a caffeine
fix.

Night vision razor-sharp, he scanned the top floor.
Ornate moldings surrounded each window casing.
Scrollwork decorated the roofline, making the old
building stand out in a neighborhood full of modern
steel and glass structures. Pretty place. Nice set-up.
Neat and tidy, without a hint of the trouble it housed
inside its storied walls. But then, appearances were
deceiving. No one knew that better than him.

Tilting his head back, he scented the air, taking
stock of the city. Wood smoke and a hint of diesel fuel
clashed with the cold, bringing the chill of winter to

quiet city streets. He glanced to his right as a large truck with *POLITI* on its side rolled past one street up. His mouth curved. Good for them. Interpol and the Oslo PD were right on time, which meant...

Time to kick it up a notch and get his arse in gear.

In search of his prey, he focused on last window of the fifth floor. Soft light bled over the stone sill. Framed by thick curtains drawn back by silk ties, a man walked past the window.

Dark hair. Medium build. Complete sociopath.

Tydrin clenched his teeth on a snarl.

Adam fucking Worth. After a month of hunting, he'd finally found the bastard.

The urge to end the arsehole—unleash hell in a stream of fire—tolled inside him. Tydrin shook his head and tightened his control. He might want to wind his dragon up just to watch the beast go, but that wasn't the plan. He'd made a promise to Ivy. Given his word to the female he couldn't live without and refused to disappoint. Now he was hamstrung—stuck between his need to kill the man and the desire to please his mate.

Tydrin rolled his shoulders, making his leather jacket creak.

The soft sound drifted along the deserted street.

He barely heard it. Eyes locked on Worth, he cracked his knuckles. He must remain patient. As much as he wanted to wipe Worth from the face of the planet, his mate's needs came first. In all things. Whatever she needed, whatever she wanted, whatever she had yet to think up, he strove to make happen. He might posture and complain, but...hell. No matter how much it chaffed him he would adhere to her wishes.

Ivy required closure. She wanted to confront the

bastard. Needed to look her former mentor in the eyes and ask him 'why?' before shit went down and Worth got what he deserved.

Turning his head, he glanced over his shoulder. The black SUV he'd left running remained where he'd parked it, alongside the curb with his mate warm and safe inside. The wipers swiped across the windshield, framing the spitfire sitting in the passenger seat.

Expression intent, Ivy leaned forward and set her hands on the dash. As her gaze met his through glass, she mouthed, "Well?"

His lips twitched.

Her eyes narrowed on him.

Tydrin swallowed the urge to smile.

Impatient wee lass. She was sitting in the car under protest. A very loud one that had started the instant he'd landed in Oslo and boosted the SUV from a nearby parking lot. Too bad for her. Although, he understood her need to be a part of tracking down Worth, Tydrin didn't want her in the open. Didn't want her cold. Didn't want her worrying. Which was why she sat in the car—grumpy, no doubt muttering about the unfairness of his edict—while he stood in the street, getting the lay of the land and eyes on the target.

Firing up mind-speak, Tydrin pinged his packmate. The only warrior to accompany him on his flight across the English Channel. *"Kruger."*

*"Got eyes on him?"*

*"Aye. Stay sharp. I'm taking Ivy in."*

Kruger growled. *"Leave her in the car, man. Be quicker tae roast his arse from where you're standing."*

Didn't he know it. *"A helluva lot more fun too, but...I promised her."*

"Your first big mistake."

"Says the male without a mate. Just wait until you've a female of yer own tae keep happy."

"Never going tae happen." The click of scales echoed through mind-speak, broadcasting Kruger's discomfort. The scrape of claws over metal sounded next as his friend shifted on his perch two buildings over. "I'm too smart tae get caught in that snare."

"The more you protest, the harder you'll fall, my friend."

"Fuck you."

"I'll pass."

Kruger snorted in amusement.

Gaze still locked on his mate, Tydrin severed the connection. As the link with Kruger faded, he flicked his fingers, asking Ivy to get out of the SUV. With a quick jerk, she popped the door open and hopped out. Her winter boots touched down. Turning the collar up on her warm coat, she jogged toward him, making footprints in the fine layer of snow. He opened his arms as she reached him. She accepted his invitation, burrowing into him, enjoying his warmth, making him feel like a giant among dragons.

Setting his cheek against the top of her head, he hugged her closer. He needed a second. A second to breathe and absorb the potency of the moment. What he was about to do for his mate felt huge, as though he was about to give Ivy something she couldn't live without.

Cupping the back of her head, he kissed her temple. "Ready?"

"Yes," she whispered, gripping the back of his jacket.

"Remember the rules?"

She nodded. "You lead. I follow. If anything goes wrong, I get behind you. Kruger comes in as back up."

"All right, then," he murmured, tucking her under his arm. "Let's go."

"Tydrin?"

"Aye, lovely?"

"Thank you. I know you didn't want me to come, but—"

"You've a right tae be here, Ivy. I understand your need tae see it through tae the end."

Tipping her chin up, she smiled at him. "I love you."

"Thank the Goddess for that," he murmured, making her laugh.

Her low chuckle tightened the muscles roping his abdomen.

Such a lovely sound and...hmm. He loved making her laugh. Adored the way her eyes sparkled. Drank in the way she looked at him when her face lit up that way.

Lucky.

He was so goddamn *lucky* to have found her. To have claimed her. To have been accepted into the warm haven of her heart. She steadied his dragon half, lightening his spirit without even trying. So aye, his precious lass was worth the sacrifice he made tonight. Worth every ounce of his restraint. Worth mountains of patience too. Now all he needed to do was stick to the plan. Give her time to confront her former friend and say her piece. All while hoping the beast seething inside him stayed in control and didn't rip Worth's head off the instant Tydrin stepped through the door.

HER HAND CLASPED in Tydrin's, Ivy stood in the hallway and stared at the apartment door. Burnished by gold, the number mounted on the wooden face mocked her, making her angrier the longer she looked at it. Her mentor was somewhere behind the fancy gold plaque, no doubt hacking something he shouldn't be anywhere near. Or selling more state secrets on the dark web to the highest bidder.

Frigging traitor. Slime-licking, snot-faced degenerate.

The guy had absolutely no conscience. How he'd fooled her so completely, she didn't know. Heck, she didn't want to think about it most days, but tonight was different. Tonight, she'd reclaim her pride and make things right. Tonight, she would help her country one last time and earn back her patriot status before she left the life she'd known for good.

Kind of strange to think of it that way.

Leaving her old life behind should have made her sad. Oddly enough, Ivy wasn't upset at all. She loved what she and Tydrin were building together. Adored the dragon warriors who called Aberdeen home and bluster of the Highland coastline. It had taken time, but now that she'd settled in, she couldn't imagine living anywhere else.

Blowing out a breath, Ivy refocused on the ornate door handle surrounded by high-gloss paint. Time to go. Here...right now...was her moment.

She needed to own it and also...

Ivy snuck a sideways glance at her mate and swallowed a huff. Yup. Definitely time to get moving. Tydrin was about to explode. Connected to him in the most elemental of ways, she sensed his dragon's impatience. His need to do violence too.

Her lips curved despite her pissy mood. Energy-fuse. How she loved the connection.

Rooted in magic, the link provided a direct line to Tydrin's thoughts—when he allowed it.

Not a sure thing, by any means. He liked to protect her, and sometimes, that meant shielding her from his dragon half's violent inclinations. Tonight, though, didn't qualify. He stood strong, sharing with her, allowing her full access. Right now, his beast was in prey mode—ready, willing and able—to shred the door and let the power of his fire loose.

Ivy hummed in happiness.

Her mate was such a sweetheart. His need to protect her so fierce he could hardly contain himself.

Shifting her grip on his hand, she laced her fingers with his, then pressed a kiss to the backs of his knuckles. He gave her a gentle squeeze. The show of support warmed her, infusing her with courage as she banged on the door.

"To hell with that." Eyes glowing bright purple, Tydrin unleashed a wave of magic. The lock clicked. Multiple tumblers turned. With a growl, he pushed the door open with his mind. "Stay behind me."

Ivy nodded.

Tydrin crossed the threshold and entered the apartment.

The sound of wood scraped over the floor. Ivy tilted her head and listened. A chair, maybe. Something rustled a second before she heard Worth's voice "What the—who the hell are you? How did you get in here?"

"Wrong question."

A pause, then a hard click...the sound of Worth closing a laptop drifted through the open door. "What's the right one?"

"Who I'm here tae protect."

Taking her cue, Ivy stepped from behind her mate's broad back. "Hello, Adam."

Brow furrowed, mouth hanging open, Worth stared at her in confusion. He blinked once, twice, clearing away his surprise. "Ivy?"

"Ah, the scumbag remembers me," she said, glancing at Tydrin. His mouth curved as he tipped his chin, giving her the all clear, telling her Worth was alone in the apartment. Walking further into the swanky pad, Ivy took stock of the living room. Plush leather sectional. Two wide-backed armchairs. Oriental rugs spread out over polished wooden floors. A sideboard with a trio of expensive crystal decanters full of amber-colored liquid to the right of an antique fireplace. "Pretty fancy digs for a guy wanted by the US government. I guess crime pays."

Anger sparked in Worth's dark eyes. "Stupid girl. This could have been you, Ivy."

"How so?"

"I wanted to bring you with me. It could have been you and me against the world, but..."

She raised a brow as he trailed off. "But?"

"You're too much of a tight ass. A super patriot...all gung-ho for the flag." He smiled. The amusement didn't reach his eyes. "You made the perfect patsy, though."

"And you're a traitor," she said, her voice so low it registered as a growl. Holding his gaze, she fisted her hands, wanting to hit the jerk so much she could hardly contain it. "You're such a dumbass. Did you think I wouldn't find you? Did you think I wouldn't clear my name? I might be a white hat hacker, but I'm second to none on the dark net. It's why you hired me in the first place." She curled her lip in disgust. "Hell, I almost feel sorry for you, but you deserve every bit of what's coming to you."

Worth sucked in a breath. "What have you done?"

"I put the blame where it belongs—on you. The FBI and Interpol are suiting up as we speak. A full breach Swat Team is just down the street," she said, as her former friend rushed to the corner window. Movements frantic, Worth scurried over to the next one, pulling at the curtains, looking for the threat. With a sound of derision, she turned toward the door. "Enjoy prison, asshole."

"Ivy—wait! Listen—"

"No. I listened to you for years. Looked up to you. Trusted you. No more." Revulsion sitting like a lump in the pit of her stomach, Ivy shook her head. It seemed like a lifetime ago instead of a couple of months. One betrayal after another. So much disillusionment. All the hurt over a man who didn't deserve her trust, never mind her esteem. Her throat clogged as she walked toward Tydrin. "I'm done, babe. Let's go."

"You sure you donnae want me tae kill him?" Expression intent, Tydrin stared at Worth. Flexing his hands, he glanced at her, a plea in his eyes. "Won't take but a moment, and well... you would make my night, lass."

Tucking a strand of hair behind her ear, Ivy huffed. Her amusement was misplaced given the situation, but...God. He made her laugh. Gorgeous, big-hearted man.

"Well, that might be fun to watch, but...no," she said, looking away from a man she'd once called friend. "Let him rot in a federal prison where he belongs."

With a grumble, Tydrin nodded, but let his need

to maim the jerk go. He took her hand instead and, with one last look around the apartment, hustled her out the door, shielding her as Worth screamed her name.

Promises of money turned into threats of death.

Ivy didn't care. Nor did she stop walking or look back. The past was over, laid to rest the moment she'd looked Worth in the eyes. And as she said goodbye to who she'd once been, she clung to Tydrin, allowing him to guide her, accepting the comfort he provided, knowing she was safe as the sound of heavy footfalls echoed up from the lobby and the FBI closed the trap, finishing what she'd started. Justice finally done. Vengeance uploaded, one hundred percent complete.

# PREVIEW: EXCERPT FROM FURY OF SHADOWS

DRAGONFURY SCOTLAND BOOK 2

# 1

EDINBURGH, SCOTLAND – PRESENT DAY

T he scent of blood thickened the night air, mixing with soupy fog along rain-soaked streets, carrying the stink along the cobbled length of the Royal Mile. Hidden inside a cloaking spell, Cyprus scanned the deserted avenue from his roof top perch. No dead bodies littering refuse-lined alleyways. Nary an unconscious human in slight. Or even a hint of a blood trail to follow.

At least, not yet.

There would be, though. The stench said all that needed saying. It was only a matter of time before he found the crime scene...and got a bird's-eye view of the carnage.

With a shrug, he resettled his wings and, shuffling left, peered over the parapet. His night vision sparked. His eyes started to glow. A pale purple wash rolled out in front of him, coating all it touched, allowing him to see in the dark as he searched dense shadows. Dragon senses dialed to maximum, he fine-tuned his sonar. A pedestrian turned onto High Street. The thud of foot-falls rang through the quiet. One eye on the male, the other on the city skyline, Cyprus watched the unsus-pecting human jog up a set of shallow steps and, keys jingling, let himself in to a flat fronting one of the busiest thoroughfares in Edinburgh.

A total tourist trap.

People from all over the world came to walk the Royal Mile and visit the Castle on the cliff. View the magnificence. Touch a piece of history. And be regaled by bloody battles and the brave Scots warriors who'd fought in each.

Cyprus glanced south. Pretty place, Edinburgh Castle. Lit by bright lights, thick stone walls glowed like a beacon in the dark, inciting creative imaginings, setting the stage for yet another long night. He shook his head and, dragging his focus from the fortress, stifled a growl of frustration. What a fucking mess. His mission should've been easier than this—than being forced to cool his heels while the rogue male he hunted played hide and seek in a busy human city.

Clenching his teeth, he shifted sideways and rounded another corner, his eyes trained on the ground below. The tips of his claws scraped the low wall as he moved. Nothing. Still no sign of the bastard...or the dead bodies.

Annoyance made his muscles tense. Combating his impatience, he rolled his shoulders. Iridescent black scales reacted to the shift, ruffling into a cascade of clickety-click-click. The jagged spikes along his spine joined the parade, clattering in the quiet. A whisper of disquiet rattled through him. The situation stank of a set-up. A well-devised trap with one purpose in mind—to draw him away from Aberdeen, into a city he didn't know well and liked even less.

"And so, the hunter becomes the hunted." Winter chill fogged his exhale, making white puffs rise in rings above his nostrils. "Clever."

Or so the bastard believed.

The rogue, though, had failed to take crucial point into account. Cyprus never engaged in anything random. He plotted and planned instead. Which explained why he'd made the trip south now, didn't it? The instant he sensed the strange male fly into his territory, he'd chosen to do what his enemy wanted—played the fool, allowed himself to be lead and followed the breadcrumbs. To what end? His mouth curved. For the hell of it. For the need to avoid layering one boring night atop another. For the sheer want of a good, claw-ripping fight.

Crouched like a cat, he leapt to the adjacent building top. The yawn of an alley flashed beneath him. His bladed tail whiplashed. The click of his scales sliced through the cold as the wind picked up, rustling the trees standing sentry over vacant sidewalks. He landed with a thump and walked along the edge, attention on the street below, the rasp of his paws against tarred roof tiles loud in the stillness.

The cacophony of sound didn't matter. Nor did it travel. He made sure of it with a murmured command, strengthening the shield of invisibility that concealed his presence from human and Dragonkind alike. Eyes narrowed, irritation rising, he looked over the raised roof edge and scanned intersecting alleyways. For what seemed like the thousandth time.

"Come out, come out wherever you are." His upper lip curled, exposing the twin rows his serrated teeth. "I want tae play."

His voice hissed through his fangs, the invitation hanging in frosty air. The acceptance he craved didn't come back. Silence reigned instead. Cyprus flexed one of his front talons. Bloody hell. The bastard was smart. Or scared shitless. One or the other, but...no way to tell until he set eyes on the warrior who'd invaded his

territory. The bold move worried him. All of Dragonkind knew to stay clear of Scotland. The land, sky,
mountains and lakes—shite, all of it, every nook and
cranny, down to the last blade of grass—belonged to
his pack, and no one crossed his border without suffering the consequences.

Immediate death by dragon claw.

He liked the sound of it. Wanted to follow through
on the promise, but with the rogue using city streets to
hide, he couldn't smoke him out without doing serious damage. The thought didn't bother him—much.
Humans, after all, thrived on misery. For whatever reason, their race enjoyed demolition and reconstruction,
so...aye. He could level an entire city block, turn it to
rubble, create new jobs, fuel their economy with one
tiny fireball. Inhale. Exhale. Crash, bang, slam. Simple. Nothing to it as long as he didn't take human lives
in the process. Big satisfaction. No guilt. The perfect
crime.

Cyprus snorted at the thought. Fire-acid sparked
from his nostrils, heating the air as he jumped to another rooftop and—

*"Anything?"*

The inquiry thumped on his mental door. Cyprus
linked in, accepting the connection with his first in
command. *"Not yet."*

Wallaig growled. *"Is the wanker really going to make
us hunt all night?"*

*"Looks like it."*

*"Christ,"* Wallaig said, pure annoyance in the soft
curse. *"Of all the nights to be away from the lair, this isnae
one of them."*

The comment made him pause mid-stride.
Cyprus's brows snapped together. *"Why?"*

*"Rannock's making Haggis for breakfast. I want to be home when—"*

A gagging sound came through mind-speak. *"Fucking disgusting. I hate Haggis."*

*"Shut yer yap, Levin,"* Wallaig snapped, his irritation redirected from the hunt to his pack-mate. *"Donnae you dare insult his cooking. If you hurt his feelings, he'll stop making—"*

*"One can only hope,"* Levin said. *"That shite smells like vomit and—"*

*"Tastes even worse,"* Kruger murmured, finishing his best friend's sentence.

*"Aye, well, think what you like, but..."* Wallaig trailed off, waited a few seconds, the threat of violence shimmering in the silence. *"If you ruin the best meal I've had in weeks, I'll make sure you suck yer next one through a straw."*

*"You'd have to catch me first, old man."*

*"Whelp,"* Wallaig said, his voice so deep he sounded past homicidal and well into satanic. Cyprus knew better. Could detect his first in command's enjoyment in every vicious syllable. Wallaig might be the eldest of their pack, but he loved a good fight—verbal or otherwise. *"I'm going to rip yer claws out and nail yer scrawny arse to the ground with them."*

Levin snorted.

Cyprus grinned. The threat wasn't a new one. Wallaig promised to de-claw one of them at least once a week. Hell, the pledge of violence was practically the male's way of saying "I love you". Shaking his head, he ignored the continued banter of his warriors—and Wallaig's vow to gut Levin like a toad and feed him is own entrails—and refocused his search. Over by the church, mayhap. The scent of blood grew stronger the closer he came to St. Giles Cathedral—to sacred ground held by priests and forgotten prophets.

His attention shifted to the crown-shaped spire atop the church. Surrounded by golden light, the High Kirk of Edinburgh glowed, pouring light onto cobblestone streets and the square butted against its front entrance. With a growl, Cyprus leapt from one building to the next, his gaze fixed on the stone walls of the cathedral. Blown by a brisk wind, the acrid smell of spilled blood spiked. He snarled, the savage sound shredding the air in front of him. Bloody hell. Could the bastard really be that depraved? Had he taken the fight to humans on holy ground?

The question circled less than a second before—

Shock made him freeze where he'd landed.

Gaze riveted to the square, Cyprus sucked a horrified breath. One second ticked into two before the true extent of the carnage registered. Goddess help him. Dead humans lay everywhere. Decapitated and delimbed, body parts strewn from the base of the statue in the middle of the quad to the church's front steps. Like a sick kind of bread trail. Or the beginnings of a grotesque human puzzle with too many pieces to fathom. He didn't want to count, but...shite. There had to be at least five—mayhap six—different humans in the mess.

"*Mother of God,*" he whispered. "*The bastard.*"

Wallaig paused mid-insult. "*Cyprus?*"

"*What's going on?*" Kruger asked, the intensity of his focus so keen Cyprus registered it from three miles away. "*What do you see?*"

"*Dead humans...everywhere,*" he said, voice gone hoarse. "*Or at least, what's left of them.*"

"*What the fuck?*" Levin growled.

The click of scales echoed inside his head.

*"We're on our way."*

*"Nay, Wallaig. Stay put."*

His first in command cursed.

Cyprus growled a warning and, gaze glued to the human casualties, leapt over the roof edge. The rush of cold air curled over his horns. Six feet from the ground, he transformed, shifting from dragon to human form. Dropping fast, he conjured his clothes. Jeans, a T-shirt and his favorite leather jacket wrapped him in warm comfort as his booted feet landed on stone. Rising from his crouch, he looked both ways, searching the empty street for humans. Nothing so far. Only one conclusion to draw—no one had stumbled upon the massacre yet. Which meant he needed to move...and it had to be now. Before someone came along and called the police, forcing him to leave.

*"Hold your positions, but be ready tae move."* He didn't want to spook his enemy. The second his warriors took flight the rogue would sense the power of his pack and run for his life. Cowards always did when faced with superior strength, so...nay. Better to keep things under wraps until he got his claws on the male. Stepping off the sidewalk, Cyprus crossed the street. *"I'm going tae take a closer look."*

*"Jesus Christ,"* Wallaig grumbled, not liking his plan. Or the fact he waited outside the three-mile maker—distance enough to avoid being detected by the enemy, too far away to be of any help if the situation devolved and shite hit the proverbial fan. *"Watch yer arse, laddie."*

*"Is the rogue gone?"* Kruger cracked his knuckles, the sharp snap echoing through mind-speak.

Cyprus shook his head even though no one could see him. *"He's still here...somewhere. I smell him. I think he may be in the church."*

In fact, he was sure of it.

He scented the bastard now. Plain as day. No need to question his dragon half. The scent trail grew more intense with every step he took. And as he stepped into the square and strode past the statue of a long-dead Duke—stepping over amputated arms and legs, skirting heads with jagged neck wounds and mutilated human torsos, boot soles splashing through puddles of human blood—the senselessness of it slammed through him. Rage burned a hole in his heart, waking the vicious urge to annihilate everything his path.

His dragon half seethed, wanting out of its cage.

Cyprus obliged, letting the killer inside him out to play as he reached the front steps of St. Giles Cathedral. He took the stairs three at a time. How dare the bastard murder innocent people in his territory. He might not like the human race, but those who lived inside his borders did so under his protection... whether they knew it or not. So aye. Retribution now belonged to him. Their deaths must be avenged and a clear message sent. No one infringed on his land. The rogue had just signed his own death warrant. All he needed to do now was find the male and complete the kill.

Continue reading Fury of Shadows. Buy it now.

## A NOTE FROM THE AUTHOR

Thank you for taking the time to read Fury of a Highland Dragon. If you enjoyed it, please help others find my books so they can enjoy them too.

**Recommend it:** Please help other readers find this book by recommending it to friends, readers' groups, and discussion boards.

**Review it:** Let other readers know what you liked or didn't like about Fury of a Highland Dragon.

**Lend it:** This e-book is lending-enabled, so feel free to share it with your friends. Sign up for my newsletter to receive new release information and other freebies. You can follow me on Facebook or on Twitter under @coreenecallahan.

Book updates can be found at www.CoreeneCallahan.com

Thanks again for taking the time to read my books!

# ALSO BY COREENE CALLAHAN

**Dragonfury Scotland**
Fury of a Highland Dragon
Fury of Shadows
Fury of Denial
Fury of Persuasion

**Dragonfury Short Story Collection**
Fury of Fate
Fury of Conviction

**Dragonfury Series**
Fury of Fire
Fury of Ice
Fury of Seduction
Fury of Desire
Fury of Obsession
Fury of Surrender

**Circle of Seven Series**
Knight Awakened
Knight Avenged

**Warriors of the Realm Series**
Warrior's Revenge

## ABOUT THE AUTHOR

Coreene Callahan is the bestselling author of the Dragonfury Novels and Circle of Seven Series, in which she combines her love of romance and adventure with her passion for history. After graduating with honors in psychology and taking a detour to work in interior design, Coreene finally returned to her first love: writing. Her debut novel, *Fury of Fire* was a finalist in the New Jersey Romance Writers Golden Leaf Contest in two categories: Best First Book and Best Paranormal. She lives in Canada with her family, a spirited Anatolian Shepard, and her wild imaginary world.

CPSIA information can be obtained
at www.ICGtesting.com
Printed in the USA
LVHW031255080222
710535LV00006B/306

9 781648 390777